Wifey's
Next
Come Up

Also by Kiki Swinson

The Playing Dirty Series: *Playing Dirty, Notorious, Playing With Fire, Playing Their Games*
The Candy Shop
A Sticky Situation
The Wifey Series: *Wifey, I'm Still Wifey, Life After Wifey, Still Wifey Material, Wifey's Next Deadly Hustle*
Wife Extraordinaire Series: *Wife Extraordinaire* and *Wife Extraordinaire Returns*
Cheaper to Keep Her Series: Books 1–5
The Score Series: *The Score* and *The Mark*
Dead on Arrival
The Black Market Series: *The Black Market, The Safe House, Property of the State*
The Deadline
Public Enemy #1

ANTHOLOGIES
Sleeping with the Enemy (with Wahida Clark)
Heist and *Heist 2* (with De'nesha Diamond)
Lifestyles of the Rich and Shameless (with Noire)
A Gangster and a Gentleman (with De'nesha Diamond)
Most Wanted (with Nikki Turner)
Still Candy Shopping (with Amaleka McCall)
Fistful of Benjamins (with De'nesha Diamond)
Schemes and *Dirty Tricks* (with Saundra)
Bad Behavior (with Noire)

Published by Kensington Publishing Corp.

Wifey's
Next
Come Up

Kiki
Swinson

DAFINA
www.kensingtonbooks.com

Chapter 1

What Happens Next?

Nick and I stood there as the truck went up in flames with my father's lifeless body inside. Before we walked away from the blaze Nick advised me to wipe my father's blood from my face with the jacket I was wearing and throw it into the fire. After I did just that, he and I turned around and walked away, and we never looked back once. We knew we had to hurry and get away from the crime scene before the officers and the fire and rescue got there. It was the only smart thing to do.

"Are you alright?" Nick asked me about half a mile into our walk away from the burn site.

"No, but I will be," I told him as we walked the long road back to the parking lot of the IHOP restaurant where we left his Range Rover. "We should've parked your truck closer, This walk is becoming too much."

"It's not that bad. We're almost there," Nick said as we both navigated down the back road of a light marsh area. Thankfully, the water levels along this road weren't deep. Allowing alligators to eat me up for dinner was not on my list of things to do tonight.

"I hope God doesn't send me to hell for what I just did," I commented.

"Just look at it as a sacrifice. Your father was creating a hostile environment and now that he's no longer around to testify against Dylan, the judge on his case has to let him go."

"You do know that that detective is going to be all over my ass once he finds out my father is dead?"

"I'm already two steps ahead of you. You're gonna have to lawyer up ASAP. That way you can prevent the officers from harassing you."

"Think I should leave town?"

"That's the last thing you should do. That'll give them all the reason to think that you had something to do with it. What you want to do is act like you're grieving. Act like you're gonna be lost without your father and they will have no choice but to believe that Kendrick ordered this hit."

"What if what you're saying doesn't work?"

"Look, just call a lawyer tomorrow and they'll make sure the police don't come within one hundred feet of you."

"I wonder what Dylan is going to say after he finds out that my father is dead and that I was the one that killed him?"

"Well, if it were me, I'd be happy as fuck. I know it took a lot for you to do that since that was your pops, but at the end of the day you and Dylan will be much happier."

"I hope Dylan appreciates what I did for him."

"Oh don't worry, he will," Nick said and then immediately after our attention was diverted by flashing light coming in our direction.

"Oh shit! Somebody called 911." I panicked. Nick grabbed me by the arm and pulled me behind a stand of trees that was big enough to hide us both.

As soon as I laid eyes on the fire and rescue vehicle and the officers that followed, I instantly felt sick to my stomach. And while standing there, the reality and gravity of the murder settled into my mind. My father was dead. Poof! Just like that, he was gone. And it was at my own hands. No one else's. Now how am I gonna ever live in peace knowing this?

"We're gonna have to get out of here fast," Nick told me after the last cop car passed us.

In a flash, Nick grabbed me by the arm again and pulled me in another direction to avoid being seen by anyone. We started walking towards a wooded area. "Wait, I don't think we should go that way," I told him, pointing in a different direction.

"Well, would you rather walk that way and risk being seen by the officers?" Nick asked me as he pointed towards the road.

I let out a long sigh. "If a snake bites me, I'm gonna kill you," I told him.

"Don't worry! I gotcha'!" He assured me.

It took Nick and I a total of seventeen minutes to get back to his truck. Immediately after we crawled inside of it, a police vehicle drove slowly by Nick's SUV. While they were driving by we noticed that there were two police officers inside the vehicle. At one point we thought that they were going to stop but then they continued to drive away. "Did you see that?" I asked him, paranoid as hell.

"Yeah, I did," he replied as he carefully started the ignition and put it in reverse. He backed the SUV out of the parking space and put it in drive. "Do you see them?" Nick asked me.

"No, I don't. But I think they drove around to the back of the restaurant," I told him, unsure about the information I was giving him.

"Well, keep your eyes open," he instructed me. But it was too late; the officers had circled back around the IHOP restaurant at a moment's notice and were able to get behind Nick's truck while he was driving away. "Fuck! They're behind us,"

Nick spat. He became very nervous and it only took a milli-second for it to happen.

Nick was a very strong-minded guy. He never allowed any-one to intimidate him, and that included Dylan. Nick was gangster as gangster could get. So to see him out of that ele-ment made me see another side of him. In a situation like this, you were always supposed to be cool. Never overreact. And never let the officers see you sweat, either. But if for some rea-son you let them see you with your pants down, just know that you're putting yourself in a risky situation.

"Whatcha gon' do?" I wondered aloud, as I continued to look forward. I couldn't let the officers see sudden movement or catch me looking back at them, so I remained calm until Nick figured out what we were going to do next.

"For right now, I'm gonna keep driving until they try to pull me over," he managed to say calmly.

"Do you think they suspect that we are the cause of torching the truck with my father in it?" I asked him. I became ex-tremely nervous about the fact that there was a possibility that we could be pulled over and arrested. I could feel my entire body vibrating with tremors. My chest was heaving up and down and I could barely move my feet once Nick told me that the officers were following us. I instantly started regretting ever killing my father and leaving his burning body in that stolen SUV. How could I be so stupid?

"If they did they would've pulled us over by now," Nick re-plied.

"Well, what do you think they're doing?"

"They're probably running the license plates on my truck."

"Are the tags on your truck legit?" I asked him.

Before Nick answered me, the officers turned on their blue-and-white lights and flipped on their sirens. "Oh my God! They know one of us killed my father." I panicked.

"Kira, calm down! They don't know anything." Nick tried

to give me a pep talk. But it didn't work. I became unraveled at the seams. I was a ball of nerves. My stomach was doing somersaults. My body was so tense it felt like I was coming down with the flu. But at the same time, I was craving a cigarette and I didn't even smoke regularly. Anything that would've calmed my raggedy nerves I would've taken it at that moment.

Nick pulled his truck over and waited for the officers to approach us. "If they try to separate us and ask us what we were doing out here, tell 'em we came to IHOP to get something to eat but got into an argument and decided at the last minute that we weren't going inside," Nick coached me.

"What if they ask me what we were arguing about?" I questioned him.

"Tell 'em the argument was about me cheating," Nick instructed me. He ran over the spiel in the nick of time. Both officers were within a few feet of the driver and passenger sides of the truck.

They drew their flashlights on us with one hand while they placed their other hands near their firearms. They were both Caucasian male police officers with chips on their shoulders. "Let me see your license and registration," the officer on the driver's side demanded.

"Sure," Nick told him and reached into the glove compartment to retrieve the registration. After he grabbed the registration, he handed it to the officer, along with his driver's license.

The officer standing on my side of the truck remained silent. He kept his eyes on me the entire time. I looked at him once and smiled. He refused to smile back.

"Officer, can you tell me why you pulled me over?" Nick wanted to know.

The officer ignored Nick's question. "Just sit tight and I will be right back," he said and then he walked away from the truck. The officer on my side didn't move a step.

My heart raced so fast my head began to hurt with a migraine. I could feel my hands trembling fiercely while the officer stood there watching Nick and I. I kept my eyes on the road in front of me. I looked at Nick through my peripheral vision a few times but neither one of us dared to talk to one another. The officer noticed that too and mentioned it. "Why are you two so quiet?" he asked us.

"I'm just . . ." I began to say but Nick cut me off in midsentence, "We just had an argument. That's why we aren't talking."

"What were you two arguing about?" The officer pressed the issue.

"I found out he's cheating on me." I lied as I turned my head to face the officer.

He gave me a weird look. "I'm sorry to hear that because you're a very pretty lady," the officer commented.

"Me too," I replied and then I turned my attention back towards the road in front of me.

The police officer peered around me so he could get a clear look at Nick. "I can't believe that you cheated on this beautiful lady," he said.

Nick turned his attention towards the officer and gave him the most sincere expression he could muster up. "I didn't cheat on her sir. Trust me, it's all just a big misunderstanding."

"How long have you two been out here?" The officer wanted to know. The question came out of nowhere. I literally wanted to piss on myself.

"Not long," Nick answered him.

"How long is not long?" The officer inquired. He turned his focus back to me. "How long have you two been out here?"

I looked at Nick hoping he'd jump in and answer the question himself. Shit, I didn't know what to say. Was this a trick question? "I don't know. Maybe twenty minutes. Maybe less." I finally said while I crossed my fingers and prayed that I said the right thing.

"Why you ask?" Nick questioned the officer, hoping he'd tell us what he knew.

The officer wasn't that stupid. He either knew what Nick was trying to do or he wanted to stay a couple steps ahead of him. "Why don't you let me ask the questions," the officer replied sarcastically.

Before the officer could say another word, the other officer reemerged from the squad car and asked his partner to meet him at the back of Nick's SUV. I swear, I was about to shit on myself. My nerves were passed frazzled; I was on the brink of a nervous breakdown. "What do you think he's saying?" I whispered to Nick.

"I don't know, so I'm gonna need you to stay calm," Nick instructed me.

I took a deep breath and exhaled. A few seconds later, both officers approached both sides of Nick's truck. The officer on Nick's side spoke first. "Sir, I'm gonna need you to step out of the vehicle."

"For what? Am I being arrested?" Nick questioned the officer.

"Sir, I'm only gonna ask you one more time to step out of the vehicle," the same officer warned.

"Listen, Officer, I'm getting out of the truck," Nick said as he reached for the door handle to open the driver's side door. "But I still need to know if you're arresting me."

"Sir, put your hands up so we can see them," The officer standing on my side of the truck yelled. He raised his gun and aimed it at Nick.

"Nick, please do what they say." I panicked as I watched the second officer walk around the front of the truck to assist his partner.

Nick slowly raised his hands and placed them on the steering wheel. The first officer opened the driver's side door with his left hand and used his right hand to aim his gun at Nick. "Step out the vehicle slowly," the officer instructed him. The second officer stood just a few feet away from his partner while he too kept his gun aimed in Nick's direction. I watched everyone closely.

"I'm getting out right now," Nick announced while he eased his way out of the driver's seat.

"Keep your hands where we can see them," the first officer yelled.

"I am. Can't you see I got 'em up?" Nick pointed out.

"Nick, please take your time," I spoke up. I couldn't afford to let these officers put a slug in Nick's back.

Nick listened to me and stepped out of the truck with no hiccups. The officer that opened the door placed handcuffs on him and escorted him to his car. While the officer carefully put Nick in the back seat of his squad car, the second officer walked back to my side of the car and instructed me to step out of the truck too. "Are there any weapons in this truck?" he asked me while he kept his gun aimed at me.

"No sir," I answered quickly.

"Step out of the SUV now. And keep your hands up so I can see them," he told me.

As instructed by the second police officer, I stepped out of the truck with my hands held high. I refused to give this officer a reason to put a bullet in my head. I've seen a lot of incidents where cops have shot people for no reason. So I wasn't gonna allow that to happen to me.

Immediately after I stepped outside Nick's truck the officer instructed me to sit on the curb near the front bumper of his squad car, so I walked over there cautiously and took at seat down on the ground. I looked inside the police vehicle to see if I could see Nick, but I couldn't. Besides being blinded by the headlights of the squad car, I was sitting too low on the ground.

"Make sure you keep your hands where I can see them," the same officer reminded me as he stood over me.

I wanted to make a sarcastic remark, but I refused to give him the satisfaction that he was ruffling my feathers. In my opinion, most cops were assholes with chips on their shoulders. They always acted like they had something to prove. Tonight was no different.

Chapter 2

Close Call

I was a nervous fucking wreck sitting on the curb watching everything unfold before my eyes. While the officer was standing a few feet away from me, I'd occasionally look at him and then turn my focus to the other officer that was talking to Nick. I couldn't hear what they were saying, but I knew it was serious.

My heart continued to beat uncontrollably. All I could think about was that Nick and I were going to be arrested for my father's murder at any second. All while Dylan was still behind bars. So who would come and bail us out? Dylan's mother or sister? Fat chance, especially if Bruce had anything to say about it.

"You look a little nervous sitting there," the officer stated.

I tried to remain calm and hold onto my composure. I knew this dumb ass officer was trying to play head games with me, but I wasn't about to let him see me sweat. "I'm not nervous at all," I told him, without even looking in his direction.

"So why are your hands shaking?" He wanted to know.

I looked down at my hands and to my surprise they were shaking. I stopped them instantly and said, "Force of habit, I do it from time to time when it's chilly outside," and then I turned my attention back toward Nick and the other officer.

"Is that the real reason?" The officer pressed the issue.
I ignored him of course.

A few minutes later, the officer talking to Nick left him sitting in the back of the police car and walked back towards the SUV. "He just gave me permission to search his vehicle." The other officer informed the officer standing next to me.

"Don't you move an inch," the officer standing next to me warned.

I didn't respond nor did I look in his direction. I kept my sights on Nick. It was hard for me to see his face while he was sitting in the back of the police car, but that didn't stop me from looking. I needed direction from him and I needed it now.

"You search the back seat and I'll search the front." The other officer instructed his partner.

"I'm on it."

I knew the officers weren't going to find anything like a gun or drugs. They were wasting their time. My biggest fear was for them to connect Nick and I to my father's murder. If for some reason they decided to take us downtown and test us for gunpowder residue, then I'm fucked.

While both officers searched every inch of Nick's SUV, a female officer radioed them. "Unit 527, are you guys still in the area?"

"Yes, this is Unit 527," The officer searching the front of Nick's truck answered.

"We need a 10-38. Got a ton of homeowners asking a lot of questions over here at the burn site."

Both of the officers searching Nick's truck looked at each other. "Whatcha think?" Officer one asked.

"It looks like they're clean, so I guess we can let them go," Officer two replied.

"Unit 450 this is Unit 527, we're 10-51," Officer one said.

"Unit 527, copy that," I heard the female officer say.

"Today is your lucky day," said the officer standing near me.

"It sure is," the other officer agreed and then he headed towards his squad car. He opened the back door and let Nick out. Seeing Nick's face made me feel such a relief. But I knew we weren't out of the woods yet. We still needed to get back in the truck and drive away before we let our guards down. And even then, that wasn't enough. Cops are sneaky as hell. I wouldn't put it past them if they hid wire-taps in Nick's truck while they conducted their bogus-ass search. I mean, why did they stop us anyway? The excuse they gave us was lame as hell. But who are we? Nobody to them. They were bogus-ass police officers and bogus-ass police officers had the authority to do anything they wanted. End of story.

After I stood up from the curb, I didn't waste any time getting back in Nick's truck. Nick got back inside his truck immediately after the officer handed him his driver's license. "Are you alright?" he asked me after he started up the ignition.

"Yes, I'm fine. But could we wait until we get to your place before we talk?" I suggested.

"Yeah, sure," he said and then he drove away from the police car.

———◆———

Nick did the speed limit the entire drive back to his apartment across town. I was a basket case, and he knew it. He didn't mention it until we walked inside his apartment and locked the door behind us. I took a seat on the sofa in the living room. "Want something to drink?" he asked me after he laid his car keys on the bar area near the kitchen.

"Whatcha got?" I wanted to know.

"Effen, Svedka, Bacardi, and I got some Patrón if you want a shot of that."

"Yeah, give me a shot of Patrón. As a matter of fact, bring me the whole damn bottle. The way I feel right now, I could probably drink the whole thing," I said.

Nick grabbed the bottle of Patrón and a shot glass and brought it over to me. He set them both down on the coffee table in front of me. Two seconds later, I had the shot glass up to my mouth, pouring every ounce of the beverage down my throat. The liquor burned my throat but it didn't stop me from pouring myself another shot. Nick got himself a beer from the refrigerator and then he took a seat on the sofa next to me. He took a couple of swallows of the beer while I downed my third shot of Patrón.

"You might wanna slow down on those shots," he suggested.

"My brain is frazzled right now and this is the only thing that's calming me down," I told him.

"But you're on your fourth shot," he replied after I poured more Patrón in my shot glass.

"I'm gonna drink the entire bottle before tonight's over," I assured him.

"I can't let you do that," he said and snatched the bottle of Patrón from the coffee table and stuffed it down in the sofa cushions next to him.

It didn't bother me that Nick took the bottle from me. The effects of the tequila were already giving me that warm and tingling feeling. My head started feeling light and it seemed like things around me were moving in slow motion. I knew then that I was high. Without further hesitation, I downed the last bit of Patrón, swallowed hard and then sat the glass back down on the coffee table. I hit my chest a couple of times with a closed fist, hoping this would curtail the burning sensation in my throat, but it didn't.

"You all right?" he asked me.

"I am now," I began to say. "There was no way you could've convinced me that we weren't going to jail tonight after those officers made us get out of your truck."

"Yeah, I thought they had us too," Nick replied.

"What was the officer saying to you while you were sitting in the back seat of his car?"

"He wanted to know how long we were in that parking lot

before they saw us. Then he asked me why I smelled like gasoline."

A ball of nerves dropped into the pit of my stomach. "And what did you tell 'em?"

"I told 'em it may have happened when I was filling up my gas tank a couple hours ago. But I knew he didn't believe me, which was why he asked me could he search my truck."

"Do you think he suspected that we had something to do with that fire? Because the other officer wanted to know if we had guns or drugs in the truck."

"He only said that to throw you off. They really wanted to find out if we had anything to do with killing your pops and setting that truck on fire."

I sat there and thought for a second and that's when it hit me that Nick was right. So from this point and moving forward, we were gonna have to be on cue if the officers approached us again.

Nick continued talking about the conversation he and that officer had while he was sitting in the back of the squad car. I heard him talking, but I couldn't tell you what he was saying if you asked me. Those four shots of Patrón had me high as a kite. And all I wanted to do was lay down and get some much need rest.

Before I realized it, I was out like a light.

When I woke up the following morning, it came with an excruciating headache. There was no doubt in my mind that I had a hangover. Ugh! I really hated those things. I should've reminded myself of what happens when you drink too much the night before. I also found myself lying on Nick's living room sofa with a warm blanket covering me. I heard Nick shuffling things around the kitchen so I called his name. "Nick, I'm in desperate need of some aspirins so my head can stop pounding," I yelled.

Nick peeped his head around the corner. "I've got some ibuprofen if that'll work," he told me.

"I'll take anything right now," I assured him.

A few minutes later, he walked out of the kitchen with a bottle of ibuprofen and a bottle of water and handed them both to me. "Thanks," I said and immediately ingested them both.

I saw Nick take a seat on the chair across from me before I laid my head back against the headrest of the sofa. I closed my eyes, believing this would help eliminate my headache faster. Boy, was I wrong.

"We're gonna have to come up with a really good alibi for when the police confront you and give you the news that your father is dead," Nick said.

"I know," I replied without opening my eyes. I wanted to pretend that everything around me was dark.

"Have you thought about what to tell 'em?" Nick wanted to know.

"Well, I know I can't say that I was home, especially after having that run-in with the fucking cops that pulled us over last night. That would be a dead giveaway. And who knows, they may even say that they smelled gasoline on you too." I pointed out.

"Don't worry about that. I'll deny it until my face turns blue. What we need to focus on is why we were in that parking lot and how long we were there."

I opened both of my eyes and looked directly at Nick. "Let's say that you picked me up to talk and thought that IHOP would be a good place to do it. But we never went inside because we started arguing."

Nick thought for a moment and then he said, "Okay, yeah, let's go with that. But if they really try to put the heat on you, call Dylan's lawyer immediately. He'll keep those motherfuckers from interrogating you."

"What if I fuck up and say the wrong thing?"

"You gotta remain calm and you'll do good."

"You make that shit sound so easy."

"That's because it is."

I sucked my teeth. "I think I should just leave town for a little while until all of this blows over."

"Kira, you can't do that. Running away would make you a primary suspect. Just go home and act like nothing is wrong. And when the officers show up to your front door and tell you that they found your father's body, you gotta fall down to your knees and act like your world just fell apart. Shed some tears if you can. And if you know how to faint, then do that too, because those fuckers are gonna be watching you really close."

It took me a several minutes to retain everything Nick said. And once my hangover subsided, it finally hit me that he was right. If I didn't go home, the cops would automatically suspect me of killing my father. So, what I had to do now was build up enough gumption to leave Nick's apartment. I knew I would eventually have to face the cops, so why not get it over with and deal with whatever they brought my way. I was a smart girl, so I would get through it.

Chapter 3

In The Nick of Time

Knots of anxiety filled up my entire stomach. Images of police officers parked outside my building or waiting at the front door of my apartment to arrest me as soon as they laid eyes on me gave me more jitters. A few times I thought about turning my car around and leaving town. But then where would I go without a dime in my pocket? The majority of my money was stashed away inside my apartment. The other small amounts of cash I had were in a couple of bank accounts I had around the city, which probably totaled up to about three grand. Now how far would that take me? No-fucking-where. My best bet was to go home like Nick said and act like everything was normal.

———◆◆◆———

I chose not to have my car valet parked when I arrived at my apartment building. I decided to park my car on my own and keep my keys in my pocket just in case I needed a clean getaway.

My heart beat faster with every step I took after I entered into my building through the garage. It felt like I was being watched for some reason but when I looked around no one was there. "Come on Kira, stop being paranoid. Just stay calm and everything will be alright," I mumbled underneath my breath.

I treaded lightly down the hallway of the floor where my apartment was located but when I was about to make a sharp right turn, I heard voices. It stopped me in my tracks. It felt like I was coming unraveled at the seams.

I stood still for a second so I could hear what was going on and hopefully find out who could be behind those voices. "Will you open the door, already?" I heard a man's voice say.

"For some reason the key seems like it doesn't want to work." I heard a woman reply. And from there, I knew it was Jimmy and his wife Molly Larson, a Caucasian hippie couple that appeared to know everything about politics. They lived across the hall from me. They weren't a threat to me, however, I didn't want to run into them for fear that they'd ask me a bunch of fucking questions about everything that was going on with Dylan, my father, and myself.

Finally after those two figured out how to open the door to their apartment, they went inside. Boy, was I relieved. A burst of energy revved up inside of me and sent me sprinting around the corner and down the hallway as fast as I could. And immediately after I got in front of my apartment door, I unlocked it, pushed it open and was inside my place in less than ten seconds flat. After I closed the front door and locked it, I felt a little better.

The feeling didn't last long because as soon as I laid my keys down on the table in the entryway of my apartment, someone started ringing my doorbell. Panic stricken, I stood still, wondering who it was. I wanted to yell and ask who was there, but my mouth wouldn't open. I even wanted to walk to the front door to look through the peephole, but once again I was too afraid to move. I feared that if I moved my feet, the person at the front door would know that I was inside.

"Kira Wade, this is Detective Grimes. Are you in there?" the detective called out. Right then and there, my suspicions were proven correct. I stood there quietly on the verge of having a mini heart attack. My hands started sweating profusely while my mind tried to figure out what to do next.

Boom! Boom! Boom! Boom! The knocks grew louder and more frequent. "Ms. Wade, if you're in there then I'm gonna need you to open the door," he belted out. Then I heard my neighbors' voices from across the hall.

"I don't think she's there," I heard Jimmy say.

"Yeah, it's been pretty quiet over there since you guys took her boyfriend to jail," Molly added.

"When was the last time you saw her?" Detective Grimes asked them.

"I haven't seen her for couple of days now," Jimmy stated.

"Well, I saw her yesterday down in the lobby getting some-one in valet to fetch her car," Molly replied.

"Do you remember what time that was?" his questions con-tinued.

"I'm really not sure. But I do know that it was sometime around six o'clock," Molly explained.

"Check with the guys in the valet. They use a daily log for all the residents in the building," Jimmy suggested.

"Thank you! I will do just that," Detective Grimes assured them.

"Hey Detective, how's her dad doing?" Molly asked.

"He was murdered last night," I heard Detective Grimes say.

"Oh my God! Really?!" Molly blurted out first.

"You got to be kidding, Detective," Jimmy added.

"No I'm not. That's the reason why I'm here. To notify her."

"What happened?" Molly wanted to know.

"Yeah, what happened?" Jimmy interjected.

"I'm not at liberty to say right now. But watch the news. You'll find that out then," Detective Grimes told them.

"Why don't you leave us your card and when we see Kira we'll give it to her and let her know that she needs to contact you," Jimmy suggested.

"All right, here you go," I heard the detective say, which indicated to me that he handed his card to my neighbors.

A few seconds later, everyone said their goodbyes and then it went completely quiet. I heard my neighbor's front door close, but that didn't mean that Detective Grimes had left the floor. And knowing that he was here to talk to me about my father spooked me. I knew one thing: it wouldn't be in my best interest to talk to that officer one-on-one. So I knew that I had to lawyer up.

I stood there for a few more seconds just to make sure Detective Grimes was gone, but it seemed like as soon as I turned around to head down the hallway towards my bedroom, I heard a rustling sound at my front door. Startled by that sudden noise, my heart nearly burst through the cavity of my chest. I turned my head back around and saw a shadow moving at my door. I immediately stopped breathing. But when I saw a small white card slide underneath the front door I exhaled. It wasn't a sigh of relief but it was close enough.

I crept toward the front door, barely making a sound and when I got close enough I kneeled down and grabbed the card from the floor. Before I looked at it I crept away from the door as quietly as I could and headed into the kitchen.

When I held that detective's business card in my hand I noticed that there was something written on the other side. I turned the card over and read his note. *Ms. Wade, please call me immediately.* I wasn't fazed by his note because there was no way I was going to call him. I mean, was he crazy? Or was he on drugs to think that I would call him? I had nothing to say to that man. He had already threatened to lock me up, and insinuated that he would throw away the key if he knew I had something to do with any of the murderers that had taken place. What I will do though, is get Dylan's attorney on the phone so he could give me the proper legal advice.

After I tossed the detective's business card on the counter-top in my kitchen, I headed to my bedroom so I could take off my clothes and take a long hot shower. Hopefully once I was done, I'd have a clearer mind.

Chapter 4

My Baby Is Coming Home

I think I stayed in the shower for at least thirty minutes. My cue to turn the water off was when the water started getting cold. I tried to think about what my next step would be concerning my father's death, but I couldn't come to terms with the fact that I had murdered him. Did that make me a bad person? Or was that a wise choice I made? I figured, whatever the case was, I eliminated my father from ratting me out to the officers, sending Dylan to prison for a long time and causing more problems by tying Kendrick and his boys to the murders of the judge, his wife and Nancy. And now that I thought about it even more, I did everybody a huge favor.

Immediately after I stepped into my bedroom I dried off, rubbed lotion all over my body and then I slipped into a pair of boy shorts and one of Dylan's white t-shirts. I sure wished that he was there right now, because I needed him to comfort me. I needed to be held by him, especially with everything going on. I guessed my time with him would come soon enough.

I lay down on my bed with my cell phone in hand and wondered what I was going to say to Dylan's attorney once I got him on the phone. With all the murders committed, it wouldn't surprise me if my cell phone was tapped, which is why I knew I needed to be very selective with my words. After mulling over how I was going to start the conversation, I finally got the gumption to dial his number.

When the line started ringing, my stomach filled up with knots. My heart started beating erratically when the phone rang for the third and fourth time. Then someone finally answered, "Thanks for calling the law offices of Berlinsky, Moss and Fentress, how may I direct your call?" A woman asked.

"Hi, my name is Kira Wade and I was hoping I could speak with Mr. Berlinsky?" I replied.

"Can I ask the nature of this call?" the woman wanted to know.

"He represents my fiancé, Dylan Callender, and I need to run a few questions by him," I told her.

"Okay, well let me find out if he's available," she said and then she put me on hold. I listened to the elevator music for about five seconds and then she returned to the line. "Hi, Ms. Wade, I'm back. I spoke with Mr. Berlinsky and he told me to tell you that he needs to see you and ask if you'd be available to stop by the office in the next hour or so?"

"Did he say what it was for? I mean, is it about Dylan?" I asked her, my mind wondering.

"No, I'm sorry, he didn't say," the woman replied.

"Can I speak to him for just a second?"

"He's on a conference call right now."

I let out a long sigh. "All right, let him know that I am on my way."

"All right. See you then."

———◆———

It took me no time to get dressed. After I slid on a pair of sneakers, a pair of sweatpants and a hoodie, I grabbed my car keys and my handbag and headed toward the front door. Before I opened it, I looked through the peephole to make sure no one was standing on the other side of the door waiting for me to come out. Once I saw that the coast was clear, I opened my front door as slowly and quietly as I could. Not only was I trying to avoid running into Detective Grimes, I was also trying to avoid seeing my neighbors Jimmy and Molly's nosy asses. I refused to give them the satisfaction of smiling in my face and laughing behind my back because of everything that had been going on. I knew they would love to ask me a bunch of questions about Dylan's situation. But that wouldn't happen, not on my watch.

Everything seemed to be running smoothly after I slipped out of my apartment and down the hallway toward the staircase, that is until one of the maintenance guys that worked and serviced my building opened the door that led to the stairs. I stumbled backwards. "Oh my God! You scared the crap out of me!" I told him while I held my hand pressed against my chest.

"I'm sorry, ma'am," he replied and then he stepped to the side, allowing me space to walk by him.

I looked at him, trying to jog my memory about where I'd seen him before. He was a young black guy. He looked like he was in his early twenties. I took a quick look at the name tag on his uniform and saw that his name was Mitchell. His name didn't ring a bell so I figured that he was a new employee. And knowing that, I knew that I was in no danger of being ratted on.

"It's okay," I finally said and then I made my way by him.

I pretended like I was going downstairs to another floor, but the moment he closed the door to the staircase, I whirled around and made a dash toward the door that led to the parking garage. I opened the door slowly and peered around the door. I scanned the entire area where my car was parked and when I saw that there were six cars out there with no one in them, I stood up and sprinted across the garage until I got to my car. I fumbled with my keys a bit, but after I calmed myself down I was able to unlock the car door and climb inside.

I started the ignition without hesitation and as soon as I put my car in reverse, I turned my body slightly to the right to look over my shoulder and out the back window and nearly had a heart attack when I saw a man standing near the trunk of my car with a hoodie covering his head.

Once he figured out that saw him, he pulled the hoodie off his head; exposing his face. I blinked my eyes a couple of times to make sure I wasn't seeing things. But after that third time, I realized that the hood-wearing perpetrator was Kendrick. He stood there like he dared me to back my car into him. I kept my foot on the brake pedal and rolled down my passenger-side window. Seeing this, Kendrick walked slowly up to the car door, placed his elbows on the window and then leaned his head in towards me.

"What's up?" I asked him. I was nervous as hell, but I refused to let him see it.

"I came by so we could talk," he said, his words barely audible. I watched him while he searched my face for a weak spot to suggest that he was intimidating me. I held my head up in a way to show him that I wasn't fazed by his presence.

"Whatcha need to talk about?" I replied in a firm matter.

"We need to talk about your father," he said.

"What about him?" I replied quickly.

"Where is he? I haven't seen him around."

"I'm sure he's probably at home."

"Come on Kira, don't play games with me," he hissed. He sounded like he was becoming annoyed.

"Kendrick, I promise you I'm not trying to play games. Just tell me what you want so I can get out here." I gritted my teeth. I was losing patience. I was also losing time sitting here when I had more pressing matters to take care of.

"So you're gonna sit there and act like you didn't set your pops on fire last night?" Kendrick replied sarcastically.

I swear, a lump instantly formed in my throat while my heart leaped from my chest. I became speechless. I didn't know whether to push him away from my car and drive away or jump out the car myself and run away as fast as I could. Unfortunately for me, neither one of those choices would've been a good one so I went with a third option and opened a small window of dialogue with him, but without incriminating myself. "Kendrick, where are you going with this?" I got up the gumption to ask.

"Let's just say that I know you and that nigga Nick hands are dirty just like mine. And I must say that that was some gangsta shit. I didn't think you had it in you." He chuckled.

I sat there in silence, while he took this moment to laugh in my face.

"Oh yeah, I just saw that detective dude leaving your building not too long ago. So, did he break the bad news to you or did he accuse you of killing him?"

"I didn't give him a chance to talk to me. When he rang my doorbell, I totally ignored it," I explained.

"Well, you know he's gonna come back, right?"

"Yes, I know."

"Well, you better get your story together or you're gonna end up in a cell next to your man," Kendrick commented and then he let out a loud chuckle.

"Don't worry, I've got everything under control," I said. By this time I was getting sick of hearing his voice. And the fact that he was talking to me like I was a child didn't make the situation any better. This wasn't my first time having a run-in with the cops. I've been down this road a few times already so I knew what I needed to do to stay a free woman.

"I'm sure you do," he said, but in a condescending manner,

and then he stood up and walked away from my car. I let out a sigh of relief after I saw him get into the passenger seat of a black, four-door Porsche truck. I couldn't see the driver because the windows were tinted. But I had a strong feeling that he had at least two to three guys in that SUV, because Kendrick never travels alone.

———❖———

I waited in the parking garage for a few minutes until I felt like Kendrick and his boys were long gone. Despite the fact that he said that he knew Nick and I murdered my father, something in my gut told me that he didn't know for sure, which was why he was in my face fishing for answers. But then again, maybe he did know. Kendrick was a mysterious guy and he loved playing mind games when he could. It gave him a sense of power. But I say, to hell with him and his manipulative tactics. And if he continued to play this game with me, I would make sure I came out as the winner.

I finally drove out of the parking garage without running into anyone else. I went straight to Dylan's attorney's office, while I looked nervously over my shoulder and through my rearview mirror. I refused to let anyone else follow me, which meant I needed to be extra careful. Not only did my life depend on it, so did my freedom.

The drive to the attorney's office was pretty emotional. I couldn't get past the fact that Kendrick and Detective Grimes had stopped by my place. Okay, I know it was Detective Grimes's job to harass me for answers that would solve the murder cases, but Kendrick was way out of line. Not too long ago he sent one of his henchmen to my building to threaten me while I was waiting by the elevator. I didn't even see that guy coming. He literally popped out of nowhere. And then today, Kendrick does the same thing. We've got to draw a line in the sand because this can't keep happening, especially with everything that's been going on. I know one thing; if things don't start turning around for the better I'm gonna have to get Nick and Dylan involved. It's simple as that.

———•◦•———

"My name is Kira and I'm here to see Mr. Berlinsky," I said to a young white woman the moment I stepped up to the reception area.

"Great! So, while you're signing in, I'm gonna let Mr. Berlinsky know that you're here." She told me and then got up and disappeared into another part of the office. About a minute later, she reappeared and took a seat at her desk. "He'll be out here to see you in a couple of minutes," she assured me.

"Thank you," I replied and then I took a seat in the waiting area. I noticed I was the only one there, which was totally fine, but for some reason I was beginning to feel alone. My father was dead and my boyfriend was in jail. So how could I correct this? How could I make my situation better? Right now, I was in a vulnerable place. If Dylan weren't in jail, none of this mess would be going on. Dylan was a fixer. He avoided a lot of things, but whenever his back was pushed against the wall, he'd get really vicious. I loved that about him. It showed me that he wasn't a man that would be pushed around. Everyone on the streets knew him so well. Kendrick was one of those people that knew how Dylan was. He hated Dylan but there was a level of respect on both sides, which brings me to a place about whether or not I should tell Dylan that Kendrick paid me a visit. Knowing how Dylan was, I knew he was going to flip out. Nothing good would come of that. So maybe I should tell Nick instead. That way he could stow it away in the back of his mind and when the opportunity presents itself, he and Dylan could handle it.

While I thought about everything that was going on in my life, Mr. Berlinsky walked into the waiting room, smiled and extended his hand, all while thanking me for coming by his office at such short notice.

"It's okay, I'm glad I stopped by because I needed to speak with you as well, but I wasn't comfortable with saying it over the phone," I explained.

"Well, come on back to my office," he instructed me, as he led the way.

Immediately after he and I sat down he said, "How are you feeling right now? Are you okay?"

Puzzled by his question, I hesitated for a second while I processed this question and then I said, "If you are referring to the fact that Dylan is still in jail, then no, I'm not okay."

"No, that's not what I'm talking about."

"Then what are you talking about?"

"I take it that you don't know," he said and then he paused.

Watching his body movement and listening to every word he uttered I knew then that he was talking about my father. But of course, I couldn't let on that I knew anything about it. If I did, and he found out later that I had not yet talked to any officers, I could become the number one suspect. So again, I had to do this thing right. I had no room for error. "Mr. Berlinsky, will you please tell me what you are talking about?" I finally said.

"Have any police officers or homicide detectives stopped by your house to talk to you today?" he asked.

"Detective Grimes stopped by my apartment not too long ago and slid his business card underneath my front door. He even put a note on the back of the card, saying that he needed me to call him. But I threw the business card in the trash. I will not allow him to continue harassing me. Those days are over."

"Listen Kira, I don't know if I should be telling you this but I feel obligated since I'm your fiancé's attorney . . ."

"Feel obligated to tell me what?" I cut him off in midsentence.

"It's being reported that your father was murdered last night. And whoever murdered him was definitely trying to send a message."

Before I said another word I knew I had to act like this was my first time hearing these facts. I also knew that if I didn't put on a show as if my heart had just got ripped out of my chest, then Mr. Berlinsky would probably look at me in a different light. So in order for me to pull this off, I thought back to when my grandmother was murdered a few years back. I left Virginia because of her. In my mind she was the only person that ever really loved me. Thinking about her instantly filled up my eyes with tears. "Please tell me you're kidding? I just spoke with him yesterday and he was fine," I said as I began to sob.

Mr. Berlinksy grabbed a couple of Kleenex from the box on his desk and handed them to me. "I'm so sorry," he said.

"Are you sure? I mean, who told you this?" I flooded him with questions.

"I saw it on the news early this morning. And when I called down to the coroner's office, they confirmed it, since I'm representing someone he filed charges against."

"What happen to him? How did he die? And where is he now?"

"All I know is that they pulled them out of a burning SUV."

"No don't tell me that! That can't be. I just spoke to him," I cried out.

Mr. Berlinsky stood up from his chair, walked around his desk and then he wrapped his arms around my shoulders. "It's gonna be all right." He tried to console me.

I laid my head against his arm and cried like I was a newborn baby. "What am I going to do?" I asked him, while I began to wipe away the tears that saturated my cheeks.

"Well, first of all we're gonna have to get you some legal counsel because if you don't call Detective Grimes back, either he or someone else is going to pressure you into going down to the station to interrogate you about your father's murder."

"Why would they do that? They know I loved my father." I continued to put on the act, while the tears continued to fall from my eyes. So far, I was doing a great job. Not only did I resemble a woman about to have a nervous breakdown, I got Mr. Berlinsky to suggest that I get legal counsel without letting on that that was really the reason why I had called him earlier. Everything was coming together perfectly.

"Don't take it personally. It's just a formality," he told me.

"Mr. Berlinsky, you know Detective Grimes hates my guts. If you recall he thinks that I'm withholding information about the murders of Judge Mahoney and his wife. So, you know he's gonna try to make my life a living hell if he gets a chance to lock me up in a room with him," I said, while I continued to sob.

"If you hire legal counsel then that won't happen. Whoever you choose to represent you will not allow a law enforcement officer to back you into a corner. So, let me make a call and see who I can get to help you," Mr. Berlinsky said and then he left my side. He walked back to the other side of his desk and reached for the office phone on his desk. I watched him as he dialed a number and put the phone up to his ear. By this time, I had toned down my sobbing. I also wiped my eyes with the Kleenex a few times when he'd glance at me. "Hey Richard," he started off saying, "I've got a young woman in my office whose father was murdered last night and the detective who's assigned to that case wants to talk to her, but I've advised her to seek legal counsel before she sits down with the police. So, do you think you'll be able to help her?"

"Sure, I'll be glad to. Ask her how soon she would be able to stop by my office?" I heard him say. The volume on Mr. Berlinsky's office phone was turned up pretty high. Before Mr. Berlinsky could repeat the other attorney's question, I nodded my head and whispered, "Where is his office?"

"His office is on the eighth floor of the Bank of America

building on Waterside Drive," Mr. Berlinsky replied after he covered the receiver with the palm of his hand.

"Tell him I can be there in fifteen to twenty minutes," I continued to whisper.

Mr. Berlinksy removed the palm of his hand from the phone and told the other attorney to be expecting me in the next fifteen minutes. After they both said their goodbyes, Mr. Berlinsky ended the call. Immediately after he hung up the phone, he looked at me and said, "I know this may not be a good time to say this, but now that your father is deceased, I can file a motion at the court clerk's office to have Dylan's case dismissed."

"Are you serious?" I asked, trying to give the impression that I was naïve.

"Yes, I am very serious."

"Does that mean he'll be getting out?"

"Yes, it does."

"So how long does this take?"

"I'm going down to the clerk's office tomorrow morning. And when I'm done filing the motion I'll give you a call," he assured me.

A few minutes later Mr. Belinsky got up from his chair and walked me out to my car. He gave me some words of wisdom that made me feel somewhat better about what was going on. "Drive carefully," he told me, and then he waved me off as I exited the parking lot of his firm.

Chapter 5

I Need to Fix This

I drove away from Mr. Berlinsky's office with a half smile on my face. One part of me wanted to celebrate the fact that my fiancé Dylan was about to come home a free man. But the other part of me felt sad because I drew blood from my father's lifeless body in order to make it happen. Some people will look at me like I was a traitor but realistically I didn't have any other choice. My father didn't think about the sanctity of my life, all he cared about was his judge friend and his wife. In my eyes, they meant more to him than I did. So guess what? It was time to eliminate the toxicity that was plaguing my life.

I couldn't stop from wondering how Dylan was going to feel once he found out that I took my father's life. He was a very protected man so I was sure he was going to thank me because my actions demonstrated how loyal I was to him. But then again, I was afraid that he would look at me differently.

Speaking of which, I started wondering why I haven't heard from him as of yet. Like clockwork, Dylan always called me every day between 8 and 9 o'clock in the morning. He would do this right after breakfast was served at the county jail. And then he'd call me back, between 11 and 12 o'clock after the correctional officers served the inmates lunch. Doing these mid-day phone calls, he'd want to know what I'd done since the first time we talked. Since I stopped working at the dealership, I had started looking after my father more, until he started acting like a fake detective. And now that that was over, I wasn't too sure how I was going to fill that void.

———◆◆◆———

Finding a parking space on Waterside Drive seemed nearly impossible. I had to circle the area five times before I found a place to park my car near the Bank of America building. It was time-consuming but I had to do it because I refused to walk a mile to get to the building.

Immediately after I entered the Bank of America building, I hopped on the elevator and went up to the 8th floor. When the elevator door opened I exited it and followed the arrows that pointed in the direction of the attorney's office, which wasn't that far. As I walked up to the glass door I noticed the attorney had his name inscribed in the middle of the glass. It read, Richard Kessler, Esq. Attorney at Law. I entered the office and a receptionist greeted me. She was a Caucasian woman. She smiled and asked how could she help me. I told her who I was and that I was there to see Mr. Kessler and before she could respond Mr. Kessler walked into the reception area. He was a short, Caucasian man with good taste in tailor-made suits. Despite the fact that he was completely bald, he was a very distinguished looking gentleman. He kind of reminded me of George Clooney with no hair. He shook my hand and said, "You are a very pretty lady."

I gave him a half smile and thanked him. He instructed me to follow him back to his office, which was down a long hallway. I peeked my head into all of the offices, from left to right while I casually walked on Mr. Kessler's heels. We finally arrived at the entryway of his office. "You can have a seat right here," he said, pointing to a leather chair opposite his desk. I

sat down and instantly looked around at all the awards and cer-
tificates he had framed and hung on the wall. To sum it up, his
office was decorated just like Mr. Berlinsky's.

"So tell me young lady, what's going on?" he asked after he
sat down in his chair.

I thought for a moment so I could gather my thoughts and
try to explain my situation without incriminating myself.
Lawyers know when someone is lying to them. They can spot a
liar a mile away. To keep it real, I was one of those liars, so I
knew I had to sound really convincing when I lay the cards
down in front of this man.

When I felt like I was ready to talk I cleared my throat and
started off by saying, "I called Mr. Berlinsky's office to check
on the status of my fiancé's case."

"What's your fiancé's name?" he interjected.

"Dylan Callender," I told him.

"Is he in jail right now?" His questions continued.

"Yes."

"What are his charges?"

"Well, what happened was he and my father got into a
heated argument and one thing led to another. The end result
is that my father was accidentally shot and my fiancé was arrested and put in jail. He was given a bail hearing but the bail
was denied because my father is a very influential retired
judge. So, when the word circulated amongst his peers that my
fiancé shot him, everyone banded together and made sure that
he couldn't get out of jail."

"What's your father's name?"

"Judge Wade."

"Hey wait a minute, that was your father who was murdered
last night?"

I nodded my head the second Mr. Kessler reminded me of
my father's demise. It was gut wrenching to hear those words
from his mouth. And before I knew it, tears started falling

from my eyes yet again. Mr. Kessler handed me a couple of Kleenex. "I'm sorry for your loss," he told me.

"I just can't believe that he's gone," I sobbed, as a piercing feeling shot through my heart. The difference between the first time I cried and now had a lot to do with guilt. This feeling of guilt also forced me to cry in front of Mr. Berlinsky.

"Does the homicide detective have any leads?" Mr. Kessler wanted to know.

"I'm not sure and that's the reason why I am here. See, a detective named Grimes stopped by my apartment a few hours ago and slid his business card underneath my front door with a message scribbled on the opposite side asking me to give him a call."

"Do you have that business card with you now?"

"No, I left it at home. But I could go back there and get it if you want me to," I offered.

"That's not necessary, I know who he is. But let me ask you this," he pressed the issue.

I sat there sobbing, waiting to hear Mr. Kessler's question. "Have you ever had contact with this detective before?"

"Yes, several times. And each time I run into him, we never see eye to eye."

"Tell me about that."

"Well, he's investigating the murders of my father's friend and his wife's death, so out of the blue, my father convinces himself that he could assist with the investigation and starts feeding Detective Grimes false leads. One time my father told the detective that the same people that killed his friend and his friend's wife kidnapped him and that I knew who they were. I became livid when Detective Grimes questioned me about it. So from that point I told him to stop soliciting fraudulent information from my father and then I told him to get lost."

"I'm assuming that didn't work."

"No it didn't, which is why I need you as my voice."

"Do you think he's looking at you as a potential suspect?"

"I'm not sure. But I do know that he's got it out for me, so he won't be nice to me once we come face to face again. He may even start harassing me. And if that happens, I wanna be able to tell him to go straight to hell."

"No, no, no, you don't want to tell him that. You could however let him know that if he wants to have a talk with you then he'll have to call me first so I can set it up. But please keep in mind that we're dealing with a homicide detective who's arrogant and overzealous. He knows the law like the back of his hand and he pushes the limits without crossing boundaries. And knowing his reputation, he will stop at nothing until he solves the case that he's harassing you about. So if there's anything I should know, tell me now so I won't be blindsided later on."

"Wait . . . you think I'm holding something back from you?"

"No, that's not what I'm saying. What I'm saying is, if there is something the homicide detectives know about then I want to know about it as well so I can prepare a defense for you. Do you understand?"

"Yes, I understand," I replied and then I fell silent to jog my memory. To be perfectly candid, there were a lot of things I was holding back. But I couldn't open up and tell this guy because I knew it would expose all the lies I'd told. I mean, let's be real. I was hiring him to keep the officers off my ass, but do you think he'd continue to shield me if he knew the whole truth? Hell no! So, guess what? I'm going to spoon feed him like a newborn baby because no one is going to fully have my back but me.

"Is there anything else I need to know?" he pressed me.

I thought for a second longer and then I said, "The only other thing I think could be crucial is, while I was at Mr. Berlinsky's office he told me that since my father is now deceased, he's going to file a motion down at the courts to have the charges that my father filed against my fiancé dropped. And the backlash that's going to come from that will certainly have Detective Grimes thinking that either myself or my fiancé had something to do with his murder," I explained and without realizing it tears started falling from my eyes again.

"I agree," Mr. Kessler stated. "But you did say that you didn't have anything to do with your father's murder, right?" Mr. Kessler added.

"Yes, Mr. Kessler, I had nothing to do with my father's murder," I said, even though I was lying through my teeth. Thankfully, the tears falling from my eyes gave off the appearance that everything I had uttered from my mouth seemed plausible, because otherwise, Mr. Kessler would've probably had his doubts.

Mr. Kessler began to watch me closely as I continued on with my act. A few times he made me feel like he was looking right through me. Then he'd change his posture by giving me a look of empathy, like he genuinely cared about me and my situation and wanted to do everything within his power to make things better for me.

"Has anyone contacted you about coming down to the county morgue to ID your father's body?"

"No."

"Well, you're going to be getting that call pretty soon so be ready."

"What if I don't get a call? Do you think it would be a good idea to go down to their office anyway?" I asked.

"Trust me, they will call you. And please be aware that Detective Grimes or another detective in his department may decide to pop in on you while you're there tying up loose ends concerning your father." He replied, as he reached towards a stack of business cards on his desk. "Here," he continued as he handed me his business card. "If anyone approaches you in uniform or in plain clothes carrying a badge, tell them you are not answering any questions without your attorney being present and then I want you to give them my card and tell them to call me," he coached me.

"Do you think that's gonna work?" I asked.

"Of course it is."

"What do you want me to do if they arrest me?"

"You said you had nothing to do with your father's murder, correct?"

"Correct."

"Well then, you have nothing to worry about. But if they try to detain you, I want you to call me immediately."

"Don't worry, I will."

"Do you have any questions for me?" Mr. Kessler wanted to know.

"How much is your retainer? And what will you charge me if things get ugly?"

"Since you haven't been charged with any crimes, my retainer will be $2,500. After I receive that amount, I will make the necessary phone calls to let the authorities know that I represent you and that I will accompany you if and when they decide that they want to speak with you about their ongoing investigation. Now as far as my hourly rate, I charge $300 an hour. My receptionist will bill you at the end of every month." He explained.

"Do you have a credit card machine? Because I can pay you now with my debit card."

"My receptionist will take your payment in the reception area. So stop there before you leave the office and she will take care of the rest," He instructed me.

Feeling a sense of relief, I stood up from my chair and shook Mr. Kessler's hand. "I wanna thank you for putting my mind at ease," I said.

"That's what I am here for."

"I guess now I can concentrate on moving forward and mourn my father's death without the officers breathing down my neck."

"Yes, you can," he agreed.

I gave him a half smile, turned around and I walked out of his office.

Chapter 6

Beyond My Control

I walked out of Attorney Kessler's office feeling a lot better than I did before I went inside. He made me feel like I could conquer anything that came my way, especially now that his retainer was paid. I poked my chest out a little bit and raised my head up high.

Immediately after I started up the ignition to my car and preceded to leave, my cell phone started ringing. I looked down at the caller ID and noticed that my baby Dylan was calling me. At this point, I was happy that I was about to talk to him, but then I realized that a lot had happened to me in the last 24 hours and I wouldn't be able to talk about it over the phone due to the fact that all phone calls from jail are heavily monitored and recorded. I went ahead and made the best of this situation.

"Hey baby," I said in a low and sad tone.

"What's up with you? Why are you sounding like that?" he wanted to know.

"Baby, there's a lot going on out here."

"Whatcha mean? Tell me what happened." He pressed the issue.

As bad as I wanted to tell Dylan what happened to my father, I knew I couldn't. In the cops' eyes, how could I know that my father was murdered if they hadn't given me the news yet? There was no doubt in my mind that the jail was recording our conversation. So whatever I wanted to say to Dylan it better not have had anything to do with my father's death, unless I wanted to incriminate myself. And since I didn't want to do that, I acted as if I had no knowledge of it. "Nothing really happened, I'm just stressed out because my dad is worrying me to death. And you're not home to help me deal with it," I finally said.

"I take it that you and he had another argument about me?" Dylan stated as if he knew what was going on.

I sighed heavily, wanting to tell him that my dad was dead and that our troubles were long gone. But once again I had to remind myself that that subject was off limits at this point. "No, I haven't talked to him in two days. And as bad as I wanna call him, I know he's gonna bring your name up and then everything is gonna go downhill from there," I explained.

"Yeah, you're right. So, how are you doing otherwise?"

I sighed heavily. "Baby, I miss you so much. And I don't know how much longer I can take being out here by myself."

"Don't talk like that, Kira. Just hang in there. Everything is going to be okay. And when I get out of this fucking jail you and I are going to take a vacation somewhere on one of those small ass islands in South America. A'ight!"

I let out another sigh. Yeah, I guess," I said.

"When was the last time you talked to my moms and my sister?"

"That's a good question because I haven't spoken to either one of them in a couple days," I told him.

"Well, I've called them both a couple of times and they never answer their phones. So I want you to call them or go over there and check on them," he instructed me.

"Okay, I'll go. But the last time I went over there, Bruce answered the door, acting all weird and told me that your mother was asleep. So I told him to tell her to call me when she gets up but she never did," I replied.

"Well, go over there again. And if that motherfucker gives you any problems, tell him he's gonna have to deal with me when I get out of here."

I let out another sigh and then I said, "Will do."

A few seconds later, Dylan switched topics and asked about his attorney. "Have you talked to him lately?"

"Yeah, I talked to him earlier," I replied nonchalantly.

"What was he talking about?"

"He basically told me that he's working hard to get you another appeal for a bail hearing."

"Fuck that bail hearing! I'm tired of wasting money on bail hearings. He needs to figure out another way to get me out of here. Your dad was shot by accident. And he needs to tell them that."

"Who needs to tell 'em?" I asked, feeling a bit confused.

"Kira, I'm talking about your pops," he told me. "Your pops need to tell them what really happened."

"Baby, can we please stop talking about that?" I pleaded. I wasn't in the mood to talk about my father. The feeling of guilt was taking over my entire body. I needed some relief so I pressured Dylan to talk about something else.

"Have you talked to Nick?" I asked.

"I called him right before I called you, but he didn't answer," Dylan replied. "Why? Have you talked to him?"

"Not since yesterday."

"What was he talking about?"

"Nothing really. He just wanted to check on me to see if I needed anything."

"Well, if you talk to him before I do, tell him I tried to call him earlier."

"Okay," I said.

Dylan and I talked for the rest of the 15-minute call and before our call was terminated, I reassured him that I loved him and that I had his back regardless of how the situation turned out. He thanked me but I could tell by the sound of his voice that he didn't think he was going to walk out of jail anytime soon. And at that moment, I wished there was a way that I could make him feel differently. Telling him that he could be coming home any day now was at the forefront of my heart. But then, what's going to happen after I tell him that? My guess was that he was going to start asking me a lot of questions. *How do you know that? Did my lawyer find a loophole in the case? Or is your father dropping the charges?* However things popped off, it wouldn't look good for Dylan or myself. So, I played smart and kept my mouth closed. I figured when the right time came, I'd be able to tell him everything.

Chapter 7

More News

Aside from the fact that guilt and shame were riding me, my emotions took a nosedive into the pit of my stomach when it dawned on me that I could spend the rest of my life in jail. Yes, I was free of the drama my dad brought on me with those murders, but now I'm feeling worse than I did when he was alive. Was I ever gonna get past this? Or was it going to haunt me for the rest of my fucking life?

While I cruised down Highway 195, it dawned on me that I really didn't have anywhere to go. I couldn't go back to my apartment for the fear of running into Detective Grimes. Not to mention, that my neighbors who lived across the hall from me would love to make a citizen's arrest. I could see those crackers calling the cops on me without blinking an eye. I couldn't have that so I called Nick to see if I could chill out at his place for a few hours while I figured out my next move.

I used my Bluetooth device to dial his number. I pressed the speakerphone function after the call started ringing. To my surprise Nick didn't answer his phone. It rang four times before the call went to voicemail. After I disconnected the line, I waited for a second or two and then I dialed his cell phone number again. This time the phone rang five times before it went to voicemail. "Hey Nick, this is Kira. Where are you? I'm trying to come by your place and chill for a few hours. We also need to talk. So, call me back."

As I continued down Highway 195, it occurred to me that I needed to call Dylan's sister and mother. Hopefully, they'd pick up and answer their phone this time.

I dialed Dylan's sister's cell phone number first. Unlike Nick's phone, Sonya's phone didn't ring at all. My call went straight to voicemail. *You reached the right person, but the wrong time. Leave me a message at the sound of the beep.* BEEP!

I disconnected the call without leaving a message and redialed her cell phone number. For the second time, it didn't ring and it went straight to her voicemail. *You reached the right person, but the wrong time. Leave me a message at the sound of the beep.* BEEP!

Frustrated, I pressed the END button and dialed Mrs. Daisy's phone number. I was relieved when her phone starting ringing. I was even happier after the call was answered. "Hello," I heard a man's voice say. I knew right off the bat the male's voice I heard was Mrs. Daisy's husband, Bruce.

"Bruce, Mrs. Daisy never called me back after I left you guys' house a couple of days ago. Will you please put her on the phone so I can talk to her?"

"She's not here."

"Then where is she?"

"I don't know where she is. She left out of here over an hour ago with Sonya."

"Well, I just called Sonya's cell phone and it's going straight to voicemail."

"Maybe you should keep trying until she answers," he replied sarcastically.

"I will. Thanks," I said and disconnected the call. The

sound of Bruce's voice made me cringe. He was such an evil ass man. And for the life of me, I couldn't figure out why he was that way. I mean, Mrs. Daisy was a very kind and beautiful lady. She'd give anyone the shirt off her back. So to have Bruce mistreating her the way he did, made me want to set his ass on fire too.

Once again I was traveling down the highway, without a clue as to where I could go and hide out for a few hours. One part of me wanted to change my course and head out west where no one would ever find me. Then I remembered Nick telling me that leaving town wouldn't be such a good idea now that my father had been murdered.

Mulling over the odds of the cops stalking my residence gave me an eerie feeling. If they were, then I was going to be in a shit load of trouble. But then, what if I was overreacting? Well, I figured the only way I'd be able to find out was by going back to my apartment.

I decided to take the next exit and make a loop around and get back on the highway and head back in the direction I was coming from. I toyed with a few ideas of how I would act if Detective Grimes caught me going into my apartment building. If he walked up to me while I strolled through the lobby, I would hand him Mr. Kessler's business card and advise him to give him a call. But if he decided to wait outside of my apartment door and throw the handcuffs on me before I was able to get inside my apartment, then I'd have to play it cool. I never allow cops to intimidate me.

Seven minutes into the drive heading back to my apartment, my cell phone started ringing again. Caught off guard, I looked at the caller ID and saw that the call was coming from Mrs. Daisy's cell phone number, so I answered it. "Hi Mrs. Daisy," I said. But I got no reply. "Hello," I said once again after pressing the speakerphone function button on my Bluetooth system. Still no response. "Hello Mrs. Daisy, are you there?" I continued and that's when I heard a little breathing on the other line. I remained quiet for a moment to see if I could hear some type of noise in the background but that didn't happen. Even the sound of breathing stopped. "Mrs. Daisy, are you there? Hello," I said once more. Sorry to say, I didn't get a response. What the caller did though was disconnect our call and the line went dead.

Immediately after the call ended, I dialed Mrs. Daisy's cell phone number back. I waited for her phone line to ring but it went straight to voicemail, so I left her a message. "Mrs. Daisy, this is Kira. I saw that you just called me. I answered the phone but you didn't say anything. I figured maybe we were having a bad connection, so when you get a minute call me back."

I got off the Seventh Street exit and made a right turn on Brickell Ave. Right after I made the turn a traffic cop flashed his lights and signaled for me to pull over to the side of the road. I swear, my heart felt like it was about to burst from my chest. "Where the fuck did this police officer come from? And why is he pulling me over?" I said to myself, biting my bottom lip. I was a nervous wreck. I couldn't think straight even if someone paid me to because all I could think about was why this man wants me to pull my car over.

I watched him in my rearview mirror as he took his time stepping out of his vehicle. At one point, I saw him speaking into the police radio he had attached to his shoulder. One part of me wanted to pull off and start a high-speed chase. But I decided against it, because I knew that wouldn't be a smart thing to do. I could end up causing a terrible car crash and I didn't want that, so I sat there and waited.

Finally after waiting for a total of one minute and a half, the officer finally approached my car. He was a very tall, Caucasian man, so he had to stoop down a little bit so he could see my face. "Officer, can you tell me why you pulled my car over?" I didn't hesitate to ask.

"Will you please hand me your license, registration, and insurance card?" he said, totally refusing to answer my question.

I grabbed my driver's license from my purse and then I took the registration and insurance card from the glove compartment and handed all three items to him.

"Remain in your car and I will be right back," he told me.

I sat in my car while anxiety slowly engulfed my entire body. For the life of me, I've always tried to do things the right way, but for some crazy reason nothing good ever comes from it. I swear, it feels like someone has put a hex on me because there's no way all of these bad things keep happening to me, and I didn't initiate them. I didn't ask for Nancy, Judge Mahoney, and his wife to be murdered. And if my father would have minded his business, I wouldn't have sealed his fate.

All the people that I just mentioned would be alive right now if they had made better decisions. I guess what they say is true, "You reap what you sow."

I believe I looked at the traffic cop through my rearview mirror at least a dozen times, wondering what the hell he was doing in his car. Unfortunately for me, I got my answer sooner than I had anticipated when I noticed another patrol car pull up and park directly behind the officer that I'd handed my driver's license to. The uniformed officer stepped out of his vehicle while the other traffic cop did the same. And instantly, my heart started beating at an unprecedented speed, all while I was still having the anxiety attack. Seconds later, I felt like I was paralyzed from the neck down. The only thing that seemed to be working was my mind. And even that wasn't working properly. Every thought I tried to hold onto disappeared before I could make sense of it. I figured the only thing I could do now was take whatever came my way and deal with it.

Once I conditioned my mind to take whatever was coming my way, I took a deep breath and then exhaled. "Come on Kira, don't let these officers intimidate you. Just let these bastards know that if they want to talk to you, then they're gonna have to contact your attorney first." I began to give myself a pep talk.

"Excuse me ma'am, but you're gonna have to step out of your vehicle," the officer who had my driver's license instructed.

"Am I being arrested?" I asked. I needed to know what was going on.

"Should I be arresting you?" he replied sarcastically.

"Will you just answer my question?" I huffed.

"Ma'am, we're only gonna tell you one more time to exit the vehicle," the other officer warned me.

"And what are you going to do if I don't?" My questions continued.

"Ms. Wade, don't give these officers a hard time. Just do what they say," I heard a male's voice say. Startled by this familiar voice, I turned my head around toward the passenger side of the car and saw Detective Grimes leaning his head slightly into the passenger-side window. He had this grimace-like expression on his face and that made me cringe instantly.

"I should've known you were lurking around one of these corners like a fucking crack-head," I hissed. I was freaking livid that these wanna-be ass patrol cops had me pulled over on the side of the road like I'd committed a crime. Well, actually I had, but they didn't know that.

"Desperate times call for desperate measures. So come on and get out of the car so we can head down to the station."

"Are you arresting me?" I asked Detective Grimes.

"Not at this moment, but I'm very confident that it will only be a matter of time before I find something on you," he responded arrogantly, smiling the entire time.

"Look, I have an attorney and he said that I am not to talk to you without him being present," I told all three men standing there.

"Who is your attorney?"

"Mr. Kessler." I said with confidence.

"Oh okay, well step out of the vehicle and then we will allow you to call Mr. Kessler so you can tell him to meet us down at the station," Detective Grimes insisted.

Before I could utter another word, the officer that had my driver's license opened up the driver's side door and waited for me to step out of the car. I couldn't think of a word to describe how angry I was at this moment. I mean, what kind of games were these guys playing? I was sick of these idiots harassing me. When would everybody leave me alone?

Finally after going back and forth with the officers, I stepped out of the car with my purse in hand and stepped to the side so the other cop could close my car door. "Kira, give one of the officers your purse," Detective Grimes instructed as he walked around the hood of my car.

"For what? You said I wasn't under arrest," I huffed. These guys were irritating the crap out of me. "You know what? I'm calling my attorney right now." I warned them as I reached inside my handbag. Before I could retrieve my cell phone, both traffic cops grabbed me and pinned me against the back door of my car. Detective Grimes snatched my purse from my hands. "Get off me," I yelled. I felt violated with these two cops manhandling me like I was a two-hundred-pound man.

"Stop resisting," Detective Grimes instructed me as he stood over me and the other two officers.

"Tell them to get off me," I snapped, struggling to get both officers to loosen their grip of my arms.

"We're not letting you go until you calm down," one of the officers said, while twisting my arms with tremendous pressure.

"I'll calm down when y'all let me go," I roared, while still resisting.

"No, you're gonna stop moving before we throw handcuffs on you," Detective Grimes threatened me. "You know you're making things harder than they need to be. I mean, all you have to do is stop resisting."

"Why don't you tell these rookie ass cops to stop twisting my fucking arm, they're hurting me!" My voice boomed.

"Fuck it! Throw the cuffs on her and put her ass in the back of the squad car," Detective Grimes demanded.

"Throw the cuffs on me for what? You said I wasn't being arrested." I yelled and screamed, while still trying to break away from them.

Before I could blink, Detective Grimes and the other two officers pushed me down to the ground, burying my face in the gravel scattered off to the side of the road. One of the officers placed plastic cuffs around my wrists. "You fucking lied to me! You said that I wasn't being arrested and that I could call my lawyer!" I said.

By this time, the tears from my eyes covered my entire face. I couldn't believe that I was being treated like a fucking animal. They zip-tied my wrists and ankles and threw me in the back of the police car. I was lying on my stomach in the back of a police car screaming frantically at these assholes about how I was going to sue the whole Miami-Dade Police Department. "I am going to make sure that all three of you clowns lose your fucking jobs because of this!"

"Good luck with that," Detective Grimes responded in a sarcastic tone, looking back at me from the front passenger seat. "Come on Sanchez, let's get out of here." Detective Grimes turned back around to face forward in his seat.

"So, you're gonna make me lie on my stomach the entire drive to the police station?"

"You left us no choice," he answered without looking back at me.

"That's bullshit and you know it," I barked, trying to hold my head up.

"Believe me, you have far more important things to worry about than lying on your stomach on the ride back to the station."

"What important things are you talking about?" I asked him.

"You'll find out soon enough," he replied.

What kind of answer was that? Was he trying to corner me with that comment? I needed to know what the hell he was talking about. Was he talking about my father? Did he have evidence that I murdered him? If he did, then why hadn't he mentioned it? Was he setting me up so I could tell on myself? Well, if that was the case then he could forget it. I'd never tell on myself. That would be the most foolish thing I could ever do. I mean, who commits a crime and then turns themselves over to the cops? No one I know. So I figured whatever Detective Grimes was talking about could not possibly have anything to do with me. I guessed now would be a good time to tell him to go and fuck himself. Better yet, I'd just let Mr. Kessler handle his stupid ass.

Speaking of which, I wasn't exaggerating when I told Mr. Kessler that this man had it in for me. He wanted me to suffer because I wouldn't help him solve his murder cases. But he didn't realize that the people who murdered Judge Mahoney, his wife, and Nancy weren't to be messed with. As soon as they found out that I helped Detective Grimes, they would kill me and everyone I loved or cared about. Kendrick and his boys were known for killing snitches. I wasn't going to give Kendrick a reason to murder me. Not in this lifetime. No way! I learned a long time ago that when you pick and choose your battles, you'll live with less stress and you'll live a lot longer.

During the rest of the drive to the police station, I didn't say another word to Detective Grimes. I refused to give him the satisfaction that he was breaking me down. Instead, I lay my head down on the back seat and closed my eyes for a moment.

Chapter 8

What Happens Next?

Upon the arrival at the police station, Detective Grimes and the police officer that was driving grabbed me and dragged me out of the back seat. They were using unnecessary force, so I snapped on them again. "Why the fuck are y'all handling me like this? I can walk, so take these plastic ass strip ties off me," I yelled.

"If you don't shut up, I will make sure that you wear these strip ties for the next twenty-four hours."

"You can't do that!" I yelled once more. "You are violating my civil rights. My attorney is going to have you begging for your fucking job after all of this is over!"

Unfortunately for me, my threats fell on deaf ears. Detective Grimes and all the other police officers stood around and smiled at me like I was a fucking joke. "Y'all think this is funny, huh? Keep laughing and I'm going to have your jobs too," I roared.

"Put her in interview room two," a plain-clothes officer told Detective Grimes.

"Roger that," Detective Grimes replied.

Interview room two was only a few feet away so it only took Detective Grimes and the other officer thirty seconds to carry me into the room and untie me. Shortly thereafter, they placed me in a chair in front of a table. There was another chair on the opposite side of the table. It didn't take long for me to figure out that that chair was going to be for Detective Grimes or some other detective on their quest to interrogate me. In my mind, it didn't matter who ended up sitting there. I was going to remain tightlipped until my attorney arrived anyway.

As Detective Grimes and the other officer walked towards the door, I asked them when they would allow me to call my attorney.

Detective Grimes slightly turned his head toward me and replied, "I'm gonna work on that now."

"Well, can I use the bathroom?" My questions continued.

"I'll get a female officer to assist you in just a few minutes," he said and then he exited the room.

I sat there quietly for a few minutes. It was a total of thirty minutes to be exact and there was not a female police officer in sight. So at that moment, I stood up from the chair, walked to the door and started knocking on it. "I need to use the restroom," I yelled from my side of the door. And of course, no one responded. I knocked on the door again. "I know you can hear me. I said I need to use the restroom," I yelled. But once again, no one responded or even acknowledged that I had said anything.

This made me really angry and that's when I started kicking and banging on the door. "I know y'all hear me! I said I need to use the restroom. I'm gonna piss on myself if you don't let me out of here."

Finally, after I threatened to urinate on the floor in that interrogation room, someone decided to open the door. I took two steps to the left, to give the person enough room so they could open the door. "I'm gonna take you to the restroom, but don't kick the door like that again," the female officer said. She was an average height and size, Black female officer with what seemed like a chip on her shoulder.

"I'm ready to go to the restroom now," I said, totally ignoring her comment.

"Let's go," the female officer said and then she escorted me out of the room.

I walked a few feet ahead of her and glanced around the entire room full of cubicles. I saw a few plainclothes detectives. And I also saw a few uniformed officers sitting in their assigned cubicles while the other ones walked around like they were actually working.

"The bathroom is right down the hall on your left," the female officer told me as she pointed in that direction. When we reached the door of the restroom she said, "I'm gonna stand right here and wait for you so don't try anything stupid."

I frowned at her and replied, "Why you acting like I was arrested?"

"Because you were," she said.

"Whatcha mean I was arrested? I didn't do anything. I was driving down the street in my car and minding my own business when your colleagues pulled me over. So how could I have been arrested for doing that?"

"I'm afraid that you're going to have to ask Detective Grimes about that."

"Where is he?" I asked, standing toe to toe with the female officer.

"He stepped out for a moment, but he will be back very soon."

"See, this is bullshit! How can I get arrested when I haven't done anything?" I snapped.

"Listen, if you don't go and use the restroom right now, I will take you back to the interrogation room," she warned me.

"I'm gonna go in there, but when are y'all gonna let me call my lawyer?"

"If you act like you have some sense, then I'll let you call your attorney when you come out of the bathroom," the officer promised me.

Feelings of relief started building up inside me. I knew I wasn't out of the woods yet, but if I played my cards right, I could call my lawyer and have him shut this whole department down.

Without further hesitation, I went inside the restroom, used it, washed my hands, and came right back out. The female officer was waiting there at the door like she said she would be. "You're still gonna let me call my lawyer now, right?" I asked.

"Yeah, so walk over to that single chair by the phone on the wall," she replied while pointing to a wooden chair placed directly underneath what looked like a payphone.

"Am I gonna have to call my lawyer collect?" I wanted to know.

"No. Just press the numbers 9-1 and that will give you a dial tone. And once you hear it, you'll be able to make your call."

As I was instructed, I pressed the numbers 9 and 1 and then I dialed the number to my attorney's office. Mr. Kessler's receptionist answered the phone on the second ring. "Thank you for calling the office of David Kessler. This is Megan speaking, how may I help you?"

"Hi Megan, my name is Kira Wade. I just left the office like an hour ago and paid you the retainer fee for Mr. Kessler."

"Yes, I remember. How can I help you?"

"Is Mr. Kessler still in his office?"

"Yes he is, but he's on a conference call at the moment. But if you tell me what you need, I may be able to help you."

"Megan, I am in police custody. And I need you to let Mr. Kessler know that I was pulled over on the side of the road for nothing. Then I was hog-tied and dragged into this police station and was just told by one of the female officers that I've been charged with a crime but she's not sure what it is. So I need Mr. Kessler to get down here ASAP."

"Do you know which station you are being held in?" Megan asked me.

"I'm at the West District Station on 142nd Avenue."

"Do you know the name of the arresting officer?" Megan's questions continued.

"It was Detective Grimes," I said, but then my attention drifted away from the conversation I was having with Megan. I heard her say something, but I couldn't repeat one word she had uttered. I became instantly distracted when I saw Detective Grimes sitting in another interview room only twenty feet away from where I was, having a fucking conversation with Nick. Now I understood why he hadn't answered his cellphone when I called him.

In my experience, before detectives start an interrogation they always closed the door to the room so the informant or suspect or person of interest would have some sense of privacy, which led me to believe that Detective Grimes kept that door slightly ajar so I would see Nick. He had planned this move. My question now was, how long had Nick been here and what had he told the detective?

"Has he tried to interrogate you or ask you any questions?" Megan asked.

"Nick what are you doing in there?" I murmured.

"I'm sorry Kira, did you say something?"

"No, I wasn't talking to you," I replied while I watched Nick closely. "Megan, I've got to go. Just tell Mr. Kessler to get down here as soon as possible." I ended the call.

I sat there quietly, trying to remember all the incidents that I'd seen Nick get into with Dylan and a few other guys and I couldn't remember one time Nick snitched. Nick had always been a straight shooter about everything. He'd always been trustworthy too. Dylan never said one bad thing about Nick.

In fact, Dylan had said many times how Nick would lay down his life for him. That's how close they are. But as I sat there and watched Nick's body language, I was beginning to see a totally different person. Nick seemed to be engaged in a heavy conversation with Detective Grimes. I even heard Nick laugh. So what was going on? Was he in that freaking room smiling in that cop's face or was I seeing things? I thought to myself while my blood boiled inside of me. Then it hit me like a ton of bricks that Nick was in there trying to save his own ass. He was in there snitching and pinning the murder of my father on me! What a fucking traitor and a bitch! Wait until I told Dylan. He was going to have Nick's head when all of this is over.

After I sat there for a couple minutes, the female officer approached me. "Are you done using the phone?" she asked.

"Yes, I'm done," I replied and stood up.

"Well, let's go," she said.

We started walking back in the direction of the interview room. Detective Grimes said something to Nick and instantly Nick whipped his head around and looked directly at me. He looked at me like he'd seen a ghost. Words could not explain the devastation I was feeling at that moment, so I put my head down and continued to walk toward interrogation room number two.

I sat down in the chair while the female officer closed the door and locked it. I lay my head down on the table in front of me and wondered what had just happened.

Hundreds of questions and assumptions scrambled around in my head, but none of them made any sense. But what stuck out more than anything was how Nick looked at me when he saw me. Was that a face of a guilty man? A traitor? A snitch? Whatever it was, I saw it with my own eyes.

While all of these thoughts were consuming me, knots started forming in the pit of my stomach and I felt a massive headache approaching. To put it plainly, I felt like I was about to have a nervous breakdown. And the fucked up part about it was that I was suffering all of this pressure on my own.

"Dylan, baby! Where are you when I need you?" I mumbled underneath my breath. I needed my fiancé there with me more than I had any other time.

I sat in the room for at least another thirty minutes before someone knocked on the door and walked in. I lifted my head up from the table and turned around only to see Detective Grimes walk into the room. He had another detective with him. "Kira, this is Detective Mann. He will be sitting in on our interview," Detective Grimes said as he closed the door to the room. Detective Mann stood next to him.

"What fucking interview? Didn't Nick tell you everything you need to know?" I replied sarcastically.

"He told me enough."

"So then why are we having this conversation?"

"Because I want to give you a chance to come clean with me. If you help me then I'll be able to help you."

"Help you how?" I hissed. "You don't give a fuck about me. All you want is to make me be your snitch just like you made my father."

"It's funny you mention that . . ." Detective Grimes said and then he paused.

"Listen, Detective, my attorney will be here in a few minutes, so I don't have anything else to say to you."

"Kira, you don't have to say another word. But I have to inform you that your father was murdered last night." He finally said it, watching my facial expression and body language the entire time.

There I was sitting down in front of these two men watching me like a pair of fucking hawks, so how was I supposed to react? What was I supposed to say? I knew I was supposed to act surprised but would it work? I mean, Detective Grimes just got through talking with Nick, so were these two trying to railroad me into a confession or what?

"That's bullshit," I replied, trying to downplay his statement.

"Stop trying to blow smoke up my ass! You know and I know that you had something to do with your father's murder!" He accused me and took a step towards me.

"My father isn't dead. Stop saying that!" I shouted.

"Cut it out, Nick already told us everything."

Before I could utter another word, the door opened and in came Mr. Kessler. I was so freaking happy to see him. I stood up and tried to embrace him, but Detective Grimes grabbed me by the arm. "You need to have a seat," he ordered me.

I snatched my arm away from him. "Keep your damn hands off me, you fucking fake ass RoboCop!"

Detective Grimes reached out to grab me again, but Mr. Kessler forced his way between us. "Detective Grimes, if you want to continue working on this police force you'd better learn how to control yourself."

Detective Grimes turned his attention toward me and then he looked back at Mr. Kessler. "I'm gonna bury your ass before all of this is over!" he threatened me.

"Have you charged my client with a crime?" Mr. Kessler asked the detectives.

Detective Grimes hesitated for a moment and admitted, "No."

"So why did that female officer tell me that I had been arrested?" I huffed. I was getting more pissed off by the second.

"Who told you that?" Grimes asked.

"Don't play dumb with me. You know who told me."

"Listen Kira, we only brought you in so we could ask you where you were last night between the hours of eight and eleven p.m."

"Don't answer that," Mr. Kessler instructed me.

"Why won't you allow her to answer the question?"

"Because I have not had a chance to brief her. Now if you'll excuse us," Mr. Kessler replied, and then he escorted me out of that interview room. I watched Detective Grimes in my peripheral vision and I could tell from his face that he was livid about the way Mr. Kessler had whisked me out of there. He'd thought he had me backed into a corner. But my attorney had rescued me.

While Mr. Kessler and I were heading toward the exit door, I remembered that the officers had my car. "Oh wait, they have my car and my car keys. I can't leave here until I get 'em."

"Okay, stay right here and I'll be right back," he told me, and then he walked back to the area where the homicide detectives were. I took a seat on a bench in the lobby. I closed my eyes and leaned my head back against the wall. Thoughts of Nick talking to Detective Grimes had me on edge. For the life of me, I couldn't figure out why Nick would sit down and kick it with Detective Grimes like they were fucking cool or something? Did he know that he screwed up the loyalty factor? If he didn't, then he was going to have to do some soul searching because once I got a chance to talk to Dylan about this, things between Nick and Dylan were going to get extremely ugly.

Mr. Kessler returned approximately five minutes later. He had my keys in hand and a document with the information about my car on it. "Here are your keys. They have your vehicle at the city impound lot. Come on, I'll drop you off."

On our way to the city impound, Mr. Kessler gave me a laundry list of things to do moving forward. "After you pick up your vehicle, I want you to go down to the county morgue so you can ID your father's body. Then I want you to go home and call a bug device specialist so they can scan your house for any surveillance devices or cameras. I can't have you walking around your apartment talking freely while the detectives can hear everything you say."

"Isn't that against the law?" I asked Mr. Kessler.

"If the police had probable cause, then they could have had a judge sign off on it," he explained.

"That's total bullshit!" I spat.

"Yes it is, so that's why I'm going to need you to do everything I tell you to do. We can't have any mix ups. Understood?"

I nodded my head.

After Mr. Kessler pulled up to the gate of the city impound lot, I sat in his car for a moment trying to figure out how I should handle the situation with Nick. "Is there something wrong?" he wanted to know.

"I saw Detective Grimes interviewing my fiancé's best friend while I was using the phone to call you."

"What's his name? And how close is he to your fiancé?"

"His name is Nick. And he and my fiancé sort of grew up together."

"Why do you think Detective Grimes interviewed him?"

"I'm not sure." I lied. I couldn't tell him that Nick was with me on the night I murdered my father. If I did that, I might as well have made the confession to the cops.

"Do you think it had something to do with your fiancé shooting your father?"

"I'm not sure, but I will find out."

"Oh no, you don't want to do that. Detective Grimes may have gotten him to cooperate. Who knows, he may be the one that murdered your father."

"I don't think he's that type of guy." I said as I reached for the door handle and opened the passenger-side door.

"You never know. If you need anything else, I'm just a phone call away."

"Thank you," I said and then I got out of his car. I went inside the impound lot's business office and got the woman behind the counter to assist me. I gave her the document Mr. Kessler had given me and after I paid her $150, she escorted me onto the grounds to retrieve my car and opened the gate so I could drive out of there.

As badly as I wanted to call Nick and curse him out, I decided that it wouldn't be a smart move, especially since my attorney had said I shouldn't do it. More importantly, I knew he was a snitch now so I figured the best thing for me to do was travel in the opposite direction away from him. At least until Dylan got home and took care of the situation.

Chapter 9

Beyond My Control

The county morgue was only a few streets away from the city impound so it didn't take me that long to get there. The moment I stepped foot out of my car, I noticed that my hands were sweating and my heart rate had picked up speed. I knew I was about to have an anxiety attack. "Come on Kira, you can handle it," I uttered to myself.

I took a couple of deep breaths, exhaled, and then I went inside the building. At the desk was an elderly white woman waiting to assist me. She smiled as I approached her. "Good evening, can I help you?" she asked me.

"Yes ma'am, I need to go to the morgue," I told her.

"You mean the coroner's office?" she corrected me.

"Yes, ma'am."

"Well, if you go down this hallway, make a right turn at the first corner, there will be a set of elevators. Go down to the ground floor and as soon as you get off the elevator the office will be on your left."

I smiled and thanked her and then I headed towards the elevator.

The elevator ride down to the ground floor was a bit shaky. It felt old and raggedy. It even made loud noises while it was moving. Thank God the ride wasn't that long because otherwise, I would've regurgitated everything I ate for breakfast.

Immediately after I got off the elevator, I went into the coroner's offices, but no one was there to greet me. There were two desks and two chairs in the waiting area but again there was no one in sight. "Excuse me, is there someone here?" I yelled, hoping this would get someone's attention. And it worked. I heard a door open and close and then I heard footsteps.

Seconds later, a middle-aged white man came from around the corner and greeted me. He was wearing scrubs, a white jacket, and a pair of Crocs on his feet. He extended his hand to me and introduced himself. "Hi, my name is Brad. How can I help you?"

"I was told by the officers that I needed to come down here to ID my father's body."

"When was your father brought in?"

"I'm assuming it was yesterday or early this morning."

"How was your father killed?"

"I was told that he was burned inside of a car," I explained.

"Okay, well follow me," he said and then he turned around and started walking back in the direction he had come from.

I followed him down the hallway and through a metal door. The metal door led to a cold room with four dead bodies lying on tables covered with white sheets. The sight of these dead people made me feel uneasy. "Why is it so cold in here?" I complained. In hindsight, I was trying to find a reason to leave out of there before the coroner got a chance to show me my father's lifeless body.

"I'm sorry about that. But the room has to be a certain temperature while I perform the autopsies."

"Will you just show me where my dad is so I can leave? I'm sorry, but this room is really creeping me out."

"Sure, he's over here," the coroner said as he pointed to the body the farthest away from the door.

As he began to pull the sheet back from my father's face, I saw how charred the top of his head was and immediately turned my head. "No, I'm sorry but I can't do this," I said. I had tears in my eyes.

"I am so sorry, ma'am."

"No, it's not your fault. You didn't know," I replied while I sobbed.

Brad walked to my side and placed his arm around me as if he was trying to comfort me. "Let me escort you back to the front office," he insisted.

After we arrived back at the front office, he handed me a few documents to sign. The first document gave the coroner jurisdiction to perform my father's autopsy. The second document stated my father's full name, date of birth, home address, that I was his next of kin, and that I would be responsible for his body after the autopsy has been completed. Once everything was established with the coroner, I got out of there as quick as I could.

———◆———

The moment I got into my car to head home a mountain of emotions consumed me. I sat there in the driver's seat and let out a flood of tears. Then I started punching the steering wheel over and over. "Why, Daddy? Why? Why couldn't you just leave shit alone?" I screamed, while trying to block out the image of the top of his charred head.

"Daddy, this didn't have to happen," I sobbed.

In that very moment, I felt like a monster. I felt like a cold-hearted bitch. The thought of my deceased mother and grandmother looking down at me and what I did made me feel really heartless.

How did I turn into this callous person? I remember once upon a time when I was a good girl. A church-going girl who made straight A's throughout school. I was also my father's little girl. Daddy's girl! We used to do everything together. Rode our bikes together. Played toss and catch. Hide and seek. You name it, my father and I did it. So to stoop down to the level where I murdered him to save myself was gut-wrenching. When would the bloodshed stop? I hoped and prayed that it ended here because I couldn't take the news of another person getting murdered. I was done.

———◆———

I wasted little time driving back to my apartment. I figured since I didn't have anywhere else to go, home would suit me just fine. I mean, it's not like I was going to hide from Detective Grimes anymore. He saw me, he said what he had to say, and now I could go home in peace.

When I pulled up to my building I started to have one of the valet guys park my car, but I changed my mind at the last minute and drove into the parking garage on my own. I wasn't in the mood to see any of my neighbors or any of the people who worked in the building. I refused to give anyone the pleasure of laughing in my face. Not today. Not ever.

Thankfully, after I parked my car in the garage no one was around. I rushed to the elevator and pressed the number to my floor. After the bell rang and the door opened, I scurried off the elevator and made a bee line to my apartment. As luck would have it though, I couldn't get into my apartment without someone seeing me.

While I was unlocking the front door to my apartment, my neighbor Molly stuck her nosy-ass head out her door. "Hey Kira, how are you?" she asked, in an annoying way.

"I'm fine. Thanks for asking," I said, while I continued to unlock the door with a key that seemed like it didn't want to work.

"I'm sorry for your loss. A detective came by your place looking for you earlier. You didn't answer your door, so he left his card with Jimmy and me," she explained while my back was still facing her.

"I've already talked to him," I replied as I continued to jiggle the front door key into the lock. Finally after forcing the key into the lock, I got it to turn and then my front door magically opened.

"Well, if you need anything I'm just across the hallway," she yelled out while I was closing my front door.

"Nosy bitch!" I hissed as I locked my front door.

I threw my handbag and car keys onto the coffee table in my living room and then I headed down the hallway to my bedroom. When I entered my bedroom, I marched toward my walk-in closet and before I could get within a few feet of it, I saw the silhouette of a man coming up from behind me. My heart nearly burst through my chest—I thought I was about to have the fight of my life. When I turned around to defend myself against what was about to happen, I was yanked up in the air with a mighty force. My feet were dangling in the air. Right before I could let out a scream, my mouth was covered with a huge hand. My yell for help was muffled. Where I was standing, I was at a disadvantage. Everything went really fast after I went into defense mode. I jerked my body back and forth while I kicked my feet hard.

A man's voice whispered in my ear. "Stop fighting, Kira. It's me. It's Nick."

I continued to kick and resist because I knew Nick wouldn't hold me the way this guy was. And why was he covering my mouth with his hand? Nick wouldn't do that either. "Kira, I need you to calm down and I'll let you go." The voice tried reasoning with me.

After I heard the guy's voice for the second time, it registered in my head that it *was* Nick, so I finally stopped resisting him. The moment he let me go, I turned around and faced him. "What the fuck are you doing in my house? And how the hell did you get in here?" I huffed. I couldn't believe that this snitch had the balls to stand in front of me after what he did earlier down at the station.

He pressed his finger against his lips and shushed me. "I think your apartment is bugged," he leaned in and whispered in my ear.

I pushed him back away from me and whispered back, "Why are you here?"

"Give me something to write with," he said.

I stepped away from him and out of my bedroom. Nick followed me to the kitchen where I grabbed a legal pad and a pen from one of the kitchen drawers. I handed them both to him. He placed the note pad on the countertop, held the pen in his hand, and started writing. He wrote a very quick note and then he slid the legal pad in my direction. The note read, "We need to talk. But we can't do it here."

I took the pen from his hand and wrote a reply. "Why the fuck do we need to talk? Didn't you say enough to that fucking cop you were laughing with earlier?"

Nick shook his head and grabbed the pen back from me and wrote, "The only reason I was laughing with him was he tried to get me to say that you and I had something to do with your pops being murdered. I told him he got his facts wrong."

"So you didn't say anything about me," I wrote after he handed me the pen again.

"Fuck no! You're like my family! I would die before I snitch on you or Dylan," his note read.

Instead of taking the pen out of Nick's hand, I embraced him. It felt good to see that Nick hadn't crossed to the other side. Now I didn't feel alone anymore. I leaned over and whispered in his ear, "Come on, let's get out of here."

Nick followed me out of the kitchen. I grabbed my car keys and handbag from the coffee table and then we both exited my apartment.

Chapter 10

Gotta Be Careful

Nick convinced me to get in the car with him when we got to the parking garage. "Those lame ass cops probably bugged your car so let's take mine," he said.

"All right," I replied and followed him to his Range Rover SUV.

After I climbed inside of the truck I buckled my seatbelt and locked my door. I can't say why I locked my door; I just did it. I think maybe I did it as a coping mechanism to help me feel safe. If that was the case, then I fully embraced it.

Once we were out of the parking garage and on the road heading to his apartment across town, Nick felt comfortable to talk. He started off the conversation by saying, "A traffic cop pulled me over and threaten to arrest me if I didn't follow them down to the police station. So I did and when I got down there, he pulled me into that interrogation room you saw me in. Then that detective walked in and started asking me all kinds of questions to see if I had something to do with your pops getting murdered. I started laughing and asked him who he got his information from because they took him for a ride."

"Well, when he came in the room to talk to me, he had me believing that you told him I had something to do with my father's murder."

"I hope you didn't buy into that bullshit."

"Don't you think that if I did, they'd still have me locked up right now?"

"True," Nick agreed. "So how did they get you?" he wanted to know.

"Detective Grimes must've put out an APB on my car because a uniformed officer stopped me and less than five minutes later, Detective Grimes showed up and hauled me down to the station."

"How did you get out?"

"I hired an attorney this morning. So after I arrived at the police station, I called him and he came and got me out."

"You know they got the surveillance tape from the IHOP spot we parked my truck in."

I was surprised by this information, and my heart rate immediately picked up. "How do you know that?" I asked.

"Because the detective told me."

"Are you serious right now?" I asked him. I couldn't believe my ears. Did Detective Grimes really have some strong evidence against me? If he did, then why did he let me go?

"Yes, I am," Nick answered.

"Well, what are we going to do?" I wanted to know.

"We're gonna go back to my apartment and come up with a plan. We've gotta stay a couple steps ahead of those fucking cops or they're gonna lock us up and give our asses a life sentence."

"I'll die first before I let those motherfuckers lock me up."

"Don't talk like that. Just let me do the thinking and the talking and we're gonna be fine. Okay?"

"Okay," I replied, enough though I wasn't totally sold on his idea.

⸻

From the moment I walked into Nick's apartment, a huge weight was lifted from my shoulders. I threw my handbag onto the sectional in Nick's living room and then I flopped down next to it. "Want something to drink? Juice? Bottle of water?" Nick asked as he headed into the kitchen.

"Yeah, a bottle of water will be fine," I told him.

While Nick was getting me a bottle of water from the refrigerator, I grabbed the TV remote and powered on the television. I sifted through the channels until I came across a local news station. A couple of seconds later, Nick came out of the kitchen with the bottle of water in hand. After he handed it to me, he sat down about two feet away from me. "We've gotta figure out a way to stay off the radar," he started off.

There was an infomercial playing so I turned my attention towards Nick. "How do you expect us to do that?" I asked him.

"First of all, we need to change phone services. Get rid of these phones we have and get new ones. And after we do that, we're gonna have to talk as little as possible on the new ones."

"Do you think Detective Grimes is going to come after us again?"

"Of course I do. So we gotta be ready when he does."

"I swear, when I saw you talking to him in that room there was no question in my mind that he had you feeding information about me."

Nick smiled. "Kira, I've already told you that you and Dylan are like family to me. There is no cop on earth that would ever get me to talk about you. I would die first before I turned into a snitch."

"Nick, I already know this, which is why I was taken aback when I saw you talking to Detective Grimes."

Nick chuckled. "I probably would've thought the same thing if I saw you sitting in there."

"It's all good. I'm just glad that we got all this ironed out now."

"Me too." He agreed and then he changed the subject. "What's gonna happen with your pops? Are you going to take care of his funeral arrangements or what?"

"Yeah, I have to. It's not like I have any brothers or sisters."

"Where do they have his body?"

"Right now, it's down at the coroner's office."

"Have you been down there yet?"

I took a deep breath and then I exhaled. "Yes, I went down there after I left the police station."

"Did you see his body?"

I hung my head low to prevent Nick from seeing the tears forming in my eyes. Nick saw anyway and scooted closer to me. "I know you're hurt," he said as he lifted my head back up and turned my face around so that he and I could have direct eye contact. By this time, I was sobbing nonstop. Nick used the backs of his hands to wipe the tears away from both sides of my cheeks. Then he wrapped his arms around my shoulders.

"Nick, when the medical examiner started pulling the white sheet away from his head, all I saw was his burnt skull, so I told him to stop. And then I walked out of there," I explained while continuing to sob.

Nick pulled me closer into his arms. "Don't worry. It's gonna be all right." Nick tried to console me.

"No, it's not, Nick, who kills their own father?" I asked him, while trying to make sense of my own actions.

"Look, I know you feel bad about it now. But time will heal your wounds."

"I can't get that image out of my head. His head looked like a ball of ashes. Just imagine how the rest of his body looked," I cried. My father's murder would probably haunt me for the rest of my life.

"Listen Kira, you got to stop blaming yourself."

"Then who else can I blame? I'm the one that lured him out of his house and told him to get in the truck. And I'm the one that pulled the trigger and set the truck on fire," I snapped and then I stood up. "I think Detective Grimes is going to find out that I killed my father." I continued. I had become extremely paranoid. I started pacing back and forth in Nick's living room.

Nick stood up and took a few steps toward me. "Kira, you're gonna have to be quiet before someone hears you. My neighbors are pretty nosy," he warned me as he grabbed me into his arms again.

While Nick tried to console me my cell phone started ringing. I was afraid to grab my phone from my handbag, so Nick did it for me. "It's Dylan," he said, holding the phone in his hand. He answered it on the third ring. "Hello," he said and he put the phone on speaker and that's when we both heard the recorded message.

"*You have a pre-paid call from Dylan, an inmate at the Miami-Dade county jail. To accept this call press one now.*" Nick pressed the one button and waited for Dylan to say hello. Two seconds later, Dylan did just that.

"Hello," he said.

Nick pulled me closer to him while he held my cell phone in his hand. "Hey baby, what's up?" I replied, trying to prevent Dylan from hearing me cry. But it didn't work. Dylan knew me like the back of his hand. He knew something was in fact wrong with me. "Are you crying?" he asked me.

"No, I had something stuck in my throat," I lied.

"Okay, well I'm calling you because my lawyer just came to see me and told me that your pops was murdered. What happened?"

"I really don't know. All I know is that he was burned up in a SUV."

"Damn! That's fucked up!"

"Yeah, I know."

"My attorney told me that you stopped by his office today too."

"Yeah, he called me and told me to stop by. He was the one to break the news to me about my father," I replied, my voice still cracking.

"Baby, are you sure you aren't crying?" he asked me again. He sounded so sympathetic.

"Yeah, Dylan, she's standing here crying. I'm trying to get her to cheer up," Nick interjected. I was glad Nick had answered Dylan's question for me. The way I was feeling right then, I probably would've told Dylan that I'd killed my father.

"Well, I got some good news," Dylan blurted out.

"What's up?" Nick asked him.

"My lawyer also told me that he was going down to the court clerk's office to file a petition for the case to be thrown out."

"That's good, baby. I'm happy for you," I managed to say, while I sobbed more than ever.

"Yeah, man, that's good to know. Can't wait to see you back out here on these streets," Nick said.

"Yeah, me too."

"Did your lawyer tell you how long it's gonna take for the motion to go through?" Nick asked.

"Yeah, he said it shouldn't take more than a week. He said he's seen motions go through in one or two days. So, that's what I'm hoping will happen in my case."

"I hope so too because you shouldn't be in there in the first place. Those fucking judges down there are just as corrupt as the cops," Nick stated.

"Yeah, they did me wrong. But I'll be alright," Dylan acknowledged. "So, have the cops been by our house to talk to Kira?"

"Detective Grimes has been harassing me on a daily basis since he locked you up," I interjected. "And I just found out that he's handling my father's murder case too. He had one of the traffic cops pull me over earlier today and then he had them take me down to the police station so he could interrogate me."

"What did he say?"

"He couldn't say much because I hired an attorney named

Mr. Kessler. And when Mr. Kessler found out I was down there, he came and picked me up."

"Well, baby, I'm sorry to hear about your father because I know you loved him very much. But look on the bright side, I should be getting out in the next few days. And once that happens, I promise I will never leave your side again. Okay?"

"Okay," I replied, my voice barely audible.

"Good. Now let me speak to Nick," Dylan instructed.

"I'm right here. Kira got you on speaker."

"Nick, take care of her."

"Don't worry. I'll look after her," Nick assured him.

"Other than that, is everything else cool?"

"Yeah, man, everything is good."

"What's up with my mother and sister? Ask Kira did she get a chance to talk to them yet?"

"Tell him no," I uttered softly.

"She said no, man. She hasn't spoken to them."

"I wonder what's going on with them."

"Me and Kira went by there sometime last week because Bruce wouldn't let Kira talk to your moms."

"Whatcha mean Bruce wouldn't let Kira talk to my moms?" Dylan asked suspiciously. I could also hear the anger reeling up inside of him.

"When Kira went by your mom's house to check on her, Bruce answered the door and told Kira that your mother was asleep and that she wasn't allowed to come inside the house. So Kira told Bruce that she had to use the bathroom and that she promised not to wake up your mom if he let her into the house."

"Did he let her in?"

"Nope. He got smart with her and told her to get off their property."

"Come on, Nick, please don't tell me that coward disrespected Kira like that," Dylan begged.

"I wish I could but that's what happened."

"Yo, Nick, I swear I'm gonna hurt that old ass man when I get out of here. I'm so fucking tired of his whack ass trying to throw his weight around that house like he bought it. My father put my mother in that damn house. Not him!" Dylan roared.

"Dylan, don't get all worked up, man. Just concentrate on getting out of there and Kira and I will handle the rest," Nick said, his intention to ease Dylan's mind.

"Do me a favor," Dylan asked.

"Sure, what's up?"

"Go by my mom's spot again. And if Bruce still won't let y'all see my mama, then call my sister, because she got a key to the house. She'll let y'all in," Dylan instructed.

"A'ight, I gotcha. I'll get it done today," Nick assured him.

"Baby, are you still there?" Dylan said through the phone. I knew he was referring to me. I was "baby."

"Yes, I'm still here," I responded. By this time I wasn't crying as much as when he first called.

"Keep your head up, baby, and this will all be over real soon. Okay?"

"Okay," I replied loud enough for him to hear me.

"I love you."

"I love you too," I told him.

Dylan and Nick talked for another twenty seconds before the phone call was disconnected at the fifteen-minute time limit. After Nick handed me my cell phone, I walked back over to the sectional, stuffed it back into my purse and then I lay down next to it. "Do you want a blanket?" he asked me.

"No, I'm fine. I just wanna lay here for a moment so I can think about my next move," I told him.

"Well, if you need anything, I'll be in my bedroom," he replied, and then he left the room.

Immediately after Nick walked out of the living room, I

snuggled up in the fetal position in the corner of the sectional and closed my eyes. Nick's entire apartment was quiet. It was so quiet that you could hear a pin drop. But as fate would have it, that small ounce of solitude went straight down the drain when I heard Nick arguing with someone on his cell phone. "What the fuck do you want now?" he roared. He sounded like he was at his wits' end.

"Bianca, I've got a lot of shit going on, so I refuse to deal with your bullshit right now," I heard Nick say. I couldn't hear anything Bianca was saying, but whatever it was it sent Nick over the edge. He started screaming at the top of his voice. "Are you fucking deaf? Didn't I just say that I wasn't dealing with your shit?" Then he fell silent.

Less than three seconds later I heard him say, "I'll tell you what, lose my number you stupid bitch!" I didn't hear anything else from that point, so I figured he hung up on her. What a way to end a conversation!

Chapter 11

A Family Affair

My mission in life was to make money, get married, have kids, and grow old with the man I love. I'd only accomplished one thing on that list, and that was getting the money. So why hadn't I been able to do any of those other things? Well, the answer was easy. With all of the drama I had come across in my lifetime, having kids would not have been a smart thing to do. Who knows, maybe one day it will happen. And then again, maybe it won't.

I wasn't aware that I had dozed off for a couple of hours until Nick woke me up. "Come on, we gotta go and check on Mrs. Daisy," Nick said as he tapped me on my shoulder.

"What time is it?" I asked, trying to get my eyes focused from the sudden light in the room.

"It's a little after five o'clock," he replied.

I rubbed my eyes with the back of my hands and then I stood up. "Don't you think we should call her first?" I asked.

"Yeah, let's call her," he agreed.

I grabbed my cell phone from my handbag and dialed Mrs. Daisy's phone number. It had been a couple days since I tried to contact her, so I was sure I'd be able to talk to her today. Unfortunately, that didn't happen, and her voicemail picked up on the first ring. I looked at Nick and said, "It went straight to voicemail."

"Call it again."

I dialed Mrs. Daisy's cell phone number again. And again, it went straight to voicemail. "It went to voicemail again," I told Nick.

"Call Sonya and see if she'll answer her phone," he suggested.

I called Sonya's cell phone number. Surprisingly, Sonya's phone rang five times and then her voicemail picked up. "Her voicemail came on so I'm gonna leave a message," I said.

"Hey, Sonya, this is Kira. I've been trying to get in contact with you for the last couple of days. When you get this message call me back." I disconnected the call.

"Something is going on with these two. I've called them a few times in the last couple days and they haven't returned any of my calls."

"Get your things and let's go over there," Nick said, and then he headed toward the front door. After I slipped on my shoes and grabbed my purse, I followed in his footsteps.

———◆———

On our way across town Nick and I didn't talk much, for fear that the homicide detectives might have bugged his truck. We did however chat a little bit about his new girlfriend. "So have you calmed down from the conversation you had earlier with Bianca?" I asked.

"Yeah, I've calmed down a little," he replied, without taking his eyes off the road.

"How long have you been dating her?" I wanted to know.

"Not long, a month maybe."

"Sounds like the honeymoon stage is already over."

"That was over after I fucked her the second time."

"What happened?" I continued to question him. I needed something to take my mind off my father's death.

"She's starting to get a little too clingy. After I slept with her for the second time, she figured she could question me about my every move. I don't do well when women try to control me."

"You should've told her that before you fucked her the first time."

"Maybe I should've. Think it's too late to do it now?" he asked me and cracked a smile.

I've smiled back at him. "Yeah, pretty much."

<hr />

The sun began to set as we pulled into Mrs. Daisy's neighborhood. For some reason, anxiety crept into my body. I tried to figure out why I was feeling like that, but my mind wouldn't let me go there. Then it came to me that we might run into Bruce again and have to deal with his shenanigans. I hoped it wouldn't happen because we already had enough shit going on.

When Nick pulled up curbside in front of Mrs. Daisy's house none of the cars were there. The driveway was completely empty. "I wonder where everyone is," Nick spoke up.

"I know Bruce sometimes works at night. Maybe Mrs. Daisy is at Sonya's apartment."

"Well, I guess that's where we're headed," Nick said as he drove away from the curb. "Try calling her again. Who knows, she may answer it this time."

I grabbed my phone from my purse and dialed Sonya's number again. I put the call on speaker so Nick could hear the conversation if Sonya answered the call this time. The phone rang six times and then the call went to voicemail. *"You reached the right person, but the wrong time. Leave me a message at the sound of the beep."* BEEP!

"Hey Sonya, this is Kira again. I just left your mother's house, but no one was home. So now Nick and I are headed over to your place. Call me back." I ended the call.

"Do you think Sonya's home?" Nick asked with uncertainty.

"I don't know, but we'll find out," I replied and then I turned my focus to the buildings and cars we passed on our way to Sonya's house. I started thinking about the choices I'd made in my life and how I'd escaped death on three occasions. During that time, I lost my husband, Ricky, my cousin Nikki, and my grandmother. I can definitely say that God has protected me all these years. Without Him, I can't say where I'd be.

Sonya lived in a townhouse only ten minutes away from Mrs. Daisy. Her neighborhood was in a middle-class area called Coral Gables. She shared the townhouse with her husband Glenn who was away in Afghanistan. Glenn and Sonya didn't have kids together, but he did have two from a previous relationship. Sonya had been very vocal about her struggle to have kids with Glenn. But she vowed to give him one before she left this earth. Sonya had the attitude of a fighter and I knew she'd never give up.

As Nick pulled his truck into the parking lot of Sonya's townhouse, we noticed that the kitchen lights were on. "I don't think she's here," I stated.

"Why you say that?"

"Because her car isn't here."

"Her car could be anywhere. I'm gonna knock on the door," Nick insisted.

I watched Nick as he got out of his truck and walked up to the front door of Sonya's townhouse. He stood there and knocked on the door a few times and then he walked over to the kitchen window that was situated near the porch. He peered through the window for what seemed like three seconds and then he turned around and walked back off the porch. Two teenage girls were standing near a tree next to

Sonya's townhouse with their eyes glued to their cell phones so Nick stopped and started speaking to them.

A minute or two later he returned to the truck and had a mouthful to say. "Those little girls are friends. One of them lives in the third house down and the other one lives across the street. So I asked them if they knew Sonya and they said they did. I asked them when was the last time they've seen her, and they said not for a couple of days."

"Maybe she's at work. She's been known to work double shifts at the nursing home," I stated.

"You think we should go up to her job?" Nick asked.

I mulled over his question for a second and then I said, "No, we don't have to do all of that. But I do think we should leave a note on her door. This way she'll know that we stopped by."

"Okay, well write a note and I'll stick it in the crack of the front door."

"I'm on it," I told him while I searched my purse for a pen and a piece of paper. After sifting through my things I found a pen and an old utility bill envelope. I flipped it over and proceeded to write the note: *Hey Sonya, where have you been? Nick and I have been looking for you. So call us! Kira.*

Immediately after I wrote the note, I handed it to Nick and watched him as he stepped out of the truck and walked back onto Sonya's porch. He opened up the screen door and slid the note into the crack near the lock. Once he secured the note he turned around and walked to the truck.

"You think the note is gonna stay in that same spot until she comes home?"

"It should. I pushed it in that crack as far as I could."

"Okay, then it should be good."

"Well, let's get out of here," Nick said as he drove away from Sonya's townhouse.

Chapter 12

What Now?

For the next couple of days I stayed at Nick's apartment. Nick insisted that I do this, at least until Dylan was released from jail. I obliged because I didn't want to be at home alone. The gruesome images of me shooting my father would not go away. I thought about it day and night. To make matters worse, I was getting one phone call after the next from the coroner's office telling me I needed to have my father's body picked up in the next few days or they would be forced to cremate him. So I got up the gumption and called Dexter's funeral home and gave them the green light to pick up his body and start funeral arrangements.

Not too long after I hung up with the funeral director, I got a call from my attorney, Mr. Kessler. I was sitting at the kitchen table with Nick eating pancakes and sausages that he'd picked up from the IHOP. I put the call on speaker so I could eat and talk at the same time. "Hello Mr. Kessler."

"Hi Kira, how are you? he replied.

"Not too good. Just got off the phone with the funeral director so I'm not in the best of spirits."

"When is the funeral?"

"In four days."

"Are you the only child?"

"Yes, I'm the only child."

"What about other family members? Do they live in the area?"

"I'm the only family member left on my dad's side. I do have a few cousins on my mother's side, but I'm not close with them at all. The last time I heard they were living in Virginia."

Mr. Kessler nonchalantly changed the subject. "Well, I called you because I got a call from Detective Grimes. He wants you and I to come down to the police station later so he can ask you more questions concerning your father's murder. So, will you be available in a couple of hours?"

"Do I have a choice?"

"Yes, you do, but I think it would be wise to go down there and answer whatever questions he may have so you can finally get this behind you."

"Can we set it up for tomorrow?" I wanted to know if I had any options.

"I have a trial coming up so I'm going to be busy for the rest of the week."

"Well, can we do it next week?" I asked, knowing I was pressing my luck.

"I don't think Detective Grimes wants to wait that long."

"I don't care what he wants," I barked. I was getting really irritated just thinking about how much of a bully Detective Grimes was. I have the right to make decisions concerning my well-being. So, if I don't want to see that whack ass cop today then I should have that option.

"I understand where you're coming from. But as your attorney I have to advise you that if you decide not to do the interview today, this is an ongoing investigation so if they find something that links you to the murder, they will come and arrest you."

"I don't care what kind of evidence they find. I love my father and I would never do anything to hurt him."

"I believe you. But I'm not the one who needs convincing."

"To hell with Detective Grimes. Tell him to leave me alone and go and find the real killer," I spat. Mr. Kessler realized that this conversation was making me upset so he found a nice way to end the call on a good note.

"I'm going to call Detective Grimes back and let him know that you're not available today because you're mourning your father. Let's see if that works."

"Perfect. I'll wait to hear back from you." We said goodbye and ended the call.

"So, that cop is trying to get you to go back down there, huh?" Nick asked between chews.

"Yeah, and you heard what I said," I replied.

"You know he's only trying to scare you into confessing."

"Yes, I know. But I'm not falling for his tactics."

"Yeah, fuck him," Nick agreed as he continued to dig into his pancakes and sausages.

I on the other hand couldn't enjoy the meal like I was before Mr. Kessler called. The mere mention of Detective Grimes had spoiled my appetite. I pushed my plate of food away from me and went into deep thought. "What's on your mind?" Nick wanted to know.

"I'm just thinking about everything that's going on. I need to go home so I can get my thoughts together," I said and stood up from the table.

"You're leaving now?"

"Yeah, I gotta get out of here."

"Are you coming back?"

"Yes, I'll be back later," I assured him and then I left.

———◦•◦———

As I was en route to my apartment, my cell phone started ringing. I hit the Bluetooth function on the dashboard and the phone number of the caller appeared. It was Mrs. Daisy so I immediately pressed the accept button and said hello, but I didn't get a response. I said hello again and she still didn't respond. "Mrs. Daisy, are you there? Can you hear me? I yelled.

Once again she didn't reply, so I disconnected the call. I started to call her back, but I figured the reception wasn't good where she was and when she got a chance she would call me back. I did send her a text a message that read, *Mrs. Daisy, your son & I are worried about you. I stopped by your house last night. I even went by Sonya's house. Give me a call please and that way we will know that you're all right.*

As soon as I sent off the text message my cell phone started ringing again. I looked at the dashboard and saw that the call was coming from Mr. Kessler, so I pressed the speakerphone function and answered his call.

"Hi Kira," he said.

"Hi Mr. Kessler."

"Okay so I just spoke with Detective Grimes, and he wants to interview you today. He also said that if we don't come in today, he's going to have you indicted on murder charges."

"Can he do that?"

"Well, so far it seems like he has a lot of circumstantial evidence against you. And with that circumstantial evidence, he would be able to get you indicted. That evidence may not hold up in court. But you don't want to go through the process of going to court to beat those charges. I think that if we go down there and talk to him, we could possibly get you cleared as a potential suspect. And then we won't have to worry about him again," Mr. Kessler explained.

Within minutes, my head started spinning and the contents of my stomach started rumbling. The mere thought of going back down to the police station and allowing Detective Grimes to interview me concerning my father's murder was not sitting well with me. I mean, what if he wanted me to take a polygraph test? What if he started questioning my whereabouts during the time my father was murdered, and I couldn't provide him with a solid alibi? I knew this guy would try to back me up in the corner, gut me like a fish, and then eat me for dinner. Hopefully Mr. Kessler won't allow Detective Grimes to do those things to me.

So after mulling over the conversation that Mr. Kessler had with Detective Grimes, I finally agreed to sit down and talk to him. "What time are we supposed to be there?"

"Would you be able to meet me within the hour?" Mr. Kessler asked me.

"I'm in the middle of something right now. But I could meet you in two hours," I told him.

"Great. Meet me in front of the station at one thirty."

"Will do," I said, and then we both ended the call.

I started to call Nick and let him know that Mr. Kessler had convinced me to talk to Detective Grimes just in case something came up and he needed to know where I was. But at the last minute I decided not to. I thought about the possibility that the cops might have my cell phone tapped, so I figured the less the cops heard me talking to Nick over the phone the better off he and I would be.

———◦•◦———

In a matter of an hour and a half, I went home, relaxed a little, and changed clothes, all before heading back out to meet Mr. Kessler at the police station. I was on my way out of my apartment when my cell phone beeped, notifying me that someone had just texted me, so I grabbed it from the inside pocket of my purse and opened the notification. The text message came from Sonya. *Kira, I've been working long shifts this past week, but don't worry I'm fine. I will call you as soon as I get a break.*

Ok, cool. Handle your business. I texted back.

Right when I was putting my cell phone away it started ringing. I looked at the caller ID and saw that it was Mr. Kessler calling me. I answered the call immediately. "Hello," I said.

"Hey, are you on your way?"

"Yes, I am. I should be there in the next fifteen minutes."

"Okay, great. See you then." Mr. Kessler said and then we ended our call.

Chapter 13

People v. Kira Wade

Mr. Kessler was waiting outside the police station like he said he would be, so I parked my car, got out of it, and scurried over to him. "Are you ready?" he asked me.

"As ready as I'll ever be."

"This is how we're gonna handle things. If the detective asks you a question that I feel might incriminate you, I will interject and cite a legal code that prohibits him from manipulating you into answering it. Or if the question makes you feel uncomfortable, then just tell him that you plead the Fifth."

"Wow! That's it?"

"Pretty much."

I took a deep breath and then I exhaled. "Well, I guess I'm ready," I announced.

"Well then, let's go."

I followed Mr. Kessler into the building and then I followed him down a very long hallway. "We're going to make a left turn at this next corner." He instructed me and then he said, "We are also going to be in the room with two detectives. They may try to intimidate you but remember I'm there so take your time when you answer their questions and again, if you're uncomfortable with it then I want you to let me know."

I let out a long sigh. "Will do," I replied, feeling really nervous.

After Mr. Kessler gave me a pep talk, we entered into the
same interview room that Nick had been in a couple of days
prior. I instantly got chills running down my spine. "After
you," Mr. Kessler said as he stepped aside so I could walk into
the room ahead of him.

"Good afternoon!" said Detective Grimes. He was sitting in
the interview room alone.

"Good afternoon," replied Mr. Kessler.

I gave Grimes the look of death and then I quickly turned
my head in the opposite direction. Quite frankly, it wasn't a
good afternoon in my eyes. It was kind of screwed up.

"Will you be interviewing Ms. Wade alone?" Mr. Kessler
wanted to know as he took a seat at the conference table. I sat
down next to him.

"No, Detective Brady will be in here in a second," Detective
Grimes stated. "Oh wait, there he is." Detective Grimes's partner walked through the door.

"I take it you guys were just talking about me," Detective
Brady said.

"As a matter of fact, we were," Mr. Kessler acknowledged,
giving him a half smile.

I watched Detective Brady as he closed the door to the room
and sat in the chair next to Detective Grimes. I looked at him
from head to toe and quickly realized that he had been one of
the detectives roaming around at my apartment the day my father was shot. He looked at me briefly and then he turned his
focus toward Detective Grimes.

"Okay Mr. Kessler, are you and your client ready to begin?"
Detective Grimes asked. He opened up a manila folder on the
table in front of him.

Mr. Kessler looked at me and asked me if I was ready. I gave him a nod even though I felt otherwise. Detective Grimes cleared his throat and started off by asking me where I was on the night my father was murdered. I looked at him and then I turned my attention toward Mr. Kessler. Was Detective Grimes serious right now? Did he really want me to answer that question so soon? I mean, the interview just started. He was seriously going for the jugular with this interview.

"Are you going to answer the question?" Detective Grimes asked me.

"What night was that?" I asked, trying to avoid answering the question.

"It was the night of the twentieth," Detective Grimes replied.

"And what day was that?" I asked, continuing to prolong the interview.

"It was Saturday night. Just four days ago," Detective Grimes explained.

"That was so long ago. I don't remember," I finally answered.

"Ms. Wade, we just had you here in the station two days ago," Detective Grimes pointed out.

"Are you sure it was two days ago? It feels like it was longer than that," I said in a nonchalant manner.

"Come on, Ms. Wade, stop bullshitting and wasting our time. We know you killed your father," Detective Brady interjected.

"I'm afraid you're wrong. I wouldn't harm a hair on my father's head," I said matter-of-factly. I tried to give the appearance that I wasn't nervous or intimidated by them.

"Well, why won't you answer the question?" Detective Brady asked.

"Which one was that?" I asked, trying to play dumb.

"We only asked you one question, Ms. Wade. Tell us your

whereabouts the night your father was murdered," Detective Grimes huffed. I could tell that he was getting extremely irritated with me.

"I don't remember," I answered.

"Well, guess what, Ms. Wade? We know where you were," Detective Grimes blurted out as he leaned on the table that separated us.

"So if you know, then why am I here?" I asked sarcastically. I was getting a little hot under the collar.

"You're here because we want to give you a chance to tell us the whole story before we draw our own conclusions. And if we have to draw our own conclusions then you're going to be up shit's creek when we're done charging and convicting you for murder," Detective Grimes stated.

"Well, I'm sorry, but I don't have a story to tell you," I told him.

"Hold that thought for a moment," Detective Grimes said and then he stood up from his seat. He walked over to the door of the interview room and opened the door. "Hey Mitchell, can you come in here for a minute?" he yelled out.

I had no idea who Detective Grimes was calling, but the thought of someone walking around the corner got me a little nervous. I heard footsteps walking towards the door and when the person appeared in the room, I instantly became sick to my stomach. "Ms. Wade, do you know this man?" Detective Grimes asked me when the man entered the interview room.

"No, I'm afraid not," I lied. But I knew the white man standing before me was one of the traffic officers who had pulled Nick and I over in front of the IHOP. I also knew that I was knee deep in shit if these officers put two and two together.

"Well, that's mighty funny because Officer Mitchell here

says that he pulled you and your buddy Nick over in the parking lot of the IHOP restaurant the night we pulled your father
from that burning SUV. Now does that little bit of information
jog your memory at all?" Detective Grimes said sarcastically.

I looked at Mr. Kessler, who by now was looking at me. I
wanted him to give me direction as to how to handle this question, but he seemed a bit clueless himself. So I turned my focus
back to Detective Grimes and Officer Mitchell. "I don't know
what y'all want me to say," I finally said, even though that didn't
make a bit of sense.

"Tell us why you and Nick were less than a half mile away
from where your father was murdered!" Detective Grimes
roared. He was irritated with me now.

"Haven't you heard of a coincidence? Because that's what
that was." I finally said.

"Why were you in the parking lot of the IHOP?" Detective
Grimes pressed the issue.

"Because we were hungry."

"What did you eat?" Detective Grimes wanted to know.

"We never went into the restaurant."

"Why not?" Detective Grimes continued his questions.

"Because we got into an argument, and I lost my appetite."

"Who got into an argument?" Detective Grimes probed
more.

"Nick and I."

"What were you two arguing about?"

"I don't remember," I lied. Nick and I had made up a story
to throw Officer Mitchell and his partner off, to prevent them
from associating us with my father's murder.

"Well, do you remember luring your father from his home
on the night that he was murdered?"

"Of course I don't."

"Why not?"

"Because it didn't happen."

"Ms. Wade, do I look naïve to you?" Detective Grimes asked me.

"I'm sorry but I don't know what naïve looks like," I responded sarcastically.

"Well let me tell you this, you and I both know that your father wouldn't have left his house with someone he didn't know. And I'm certain he wouldn't have opened his door to a stranger. So tell us, why did you do it?"

"I didn't do anything," I snapped. These cops were really trying to railroad me into confessing to my father's murder. Whether they knew it or not, I would take this lie to my grave.

"Well then, tell us who did it. Was it Nick?"

"I'm telling you guys right now that you're interrogating the wrong person."

"Tell us who we should interrogate. Give us a name." Detective Grimes continued to press me for answers to his questions.

I let out a long sigh. "I don't know."

"Oh, you know. So give us the goods."

Frustrated by the interrogation, I looked at my attorney and said, "I've had enough of this. Can we leave now?"

"Tell us why your father's body was in the back seat of that burning SUV," Detective Grimes blurted out, refusing to let Mr. Kessler respond to my question. "Whoever lured him out of his house instructed him to get in the back seat. So that means there were two people with him that night. One person was driving and the other person sat next to him in the back seat. And if you remember, Officer Mitchell can personally ID you and Nick sitting in Nick's truck less than half a mile from where the murder took place."

"Sounds like you've got this whole thing figured out."

"Not quite, but it's coming together."

"Good for you. Now can we go now?" I turned around and faced my attorney again.

"Are you charging my client with any crime?" Mr. Kessler asked. His demeanor was that of a very confident man who was ready to go to war for me.

Officer Mitchell and the other detective looked at Detective Grimes. "Let me just say that if your client leaves here today without assisting me and my partner with this murder investigation, then I won't cut her a deal and I'm gonna push for her to get life in prison without parole after I get a grand jury to indict her."

"Why don't you do that, and we'll see you in court." Mr. Kessler said. He stood up and I stood up next to him. "The only things you have right now are circumstantial evidence and coincidence, and those aren't gonna fly in court."

After Mr. Kessler dared them to try to indict me, I looked at all of them and smiled. A few seconds later, Mr. Kessler grabbed his briefcase from the table and looked at me and said, "Let's get out of here."

"I'm sorry, you guys couldn't get the information you were looking for. But I already told y'all that you were talking to the wrong person," I said as I followed my attorney toward the door.

"Who should we be talking to, Kira?"

"You guys just don't let up, do you?" I said, while I walked by them to get to the door.

"Not when we feel strongly about something."

"Well, don't let me hold you up from finding the real killer."

"I think we already have, considering we just pulled a fresh new set of your fingerprints from the doorknob on the front door of your father's home," Detective Grimes said, while I was walking out of the interview room.

I stopped in my tracks as I stepped over the entryway of the door and said, "For your information, I have a key to my father's house so quite naturally my fingerprints would be there."

"Tell us when was the last time you were at your father's home," Detective Brady asked.

I looked at him and smiled. "I don't remember," I told him and then I walked out with my attorney in tow.

Chapter 14

I'm Watching You

Going back down to the police station wasn't something I wanted to do. But I did it anyway. Thankfully, Mr. Kessler shut those cops down because if he hadn't Detective Grimes and those other two officers would've railroaded me and I would have ended the day in jail.

"I'm so glad that's over," I said as soon as we stepped outside of the building.

"I am too. For a minute there, I thought you were going to say the wrong thing," Mr. Kessler replied.

"I know. I saw your expression change a few times when it was time for me to talk," I said.

"Well, you see how badly they want to charge you with your father's murder. And the fact that they know two people were involved in his murder is a key point for this investigation. Speaking of which, why didn't you tell me that you were pulled over less than a half a mile from the murder scene?"

"Because I didn't think it was important," I lied. The real reason I didn't tell Mr. Kessler we were pulled over by that officer was because I had no idea that Detective Grimes was going to find out since there was no traffic ticket issued.

"Are you being straightforward with me? Now remember I'm on your side," he pressed me.

"Yes, I am," I tried to reassure him, but I don't think he believed me.

"Well, tell me exactly when was the last time you were at your father's house?" His questions continued.

"I'm not really sure. But it wasn't too long after he got out of the hospital," I replied, trying to give him the most sincere expression I could muster up.

"I'll tell you what, try to figure out exactly when you were at your father's house because it's important that we establish a timeline so those detectives can rule you out as a suspect."

"Okay. I can do that."

"All right, now be careful. Don't talk to anyone while this investigation is going on. Do I make myself clear?"

"Absolutely."

"And don't forget to call me if you need anything."

"I will," I replied as we shook hands and then we parted ways.

———— ◦◦◦ ————

It felt like a weight had been lifted from my shoulders once the interrogation was over. Detective Grimes certainly tried to railroad me when he brought that traffic cop into the interrogation room. I know one thing, if that traffic cop had tested my hands for gunpowder I would have ended up in from of a judge at a bail hearing. If you are arrested for murder in the state of Florida, the justice system will try to throw the book at you. And if the murder victim was a well-respected judge like my father was, his peers in the court system will try to give you the death penalty. I can't have that. No way.

After I sat down in the driver's seat of my car, I watched Mr. Kessler drive away. Driving a $150,000 late-model Porsche sent a clear message that he was living the good life. I couldn't tell you how peaceful his life was, but if he was charging all of his clients the amount of money he charged me, he was a very

rich man, and rich men buy peace and happiness all the time.
It's the way of the world.

When I started up the ignition, I realized that I needed to
full up my car. The gas tank was almost on empty so I drove to
the nearest gas station, which was only three blocks away from
the police station. I took my debit card out of my purse and
stepped out of the car. I stepped up to the gas pump, swiped
my card, and once I was authorized to pump the gas I took the
hose and started filling my tank.

While I was pumping the gas into my car, I couldn't help
but wonder if Detective Grimes was telling the truth when he
mentioned that the forensic detectives had pulled fresh fingerprints that belonged to me from my father's doorknob. I mean,
how fresh could they have been? And was there really a thing
called fresh fingerprints?

Like I said to the detective, I had a key to my father's house
so whether the fingerprints were new or not, they really had no
evidence that implicated me as being the murderer. I had been
caught off guard when Detective Grimes stated that they knew
that there had to be at least two killers because my father was
sitting in the back seat of the truck. I almost had a heart attack
when he mentioned that. But thankfully my attorney was present, and he saved me every time he felt he needed to. I guess I
can say that was money well spent.

The gas meter stopped at $35 and while I was putting the
hose back into the gas pump, a car pulled up behind me. I
looked over my shoulder and saw two men sitting in the front
seat. I recognized both men, but I only knew the name of the
man in the passenger seat.

I forced a smile as I waved at him. "Hey Kendrick, what's
up?" I asked while I walked slowly towards the car.

Kendrick leaned his head out the passenger-side window.
"Chilling," he replied as he watched me approach him.

Anxiety crept inside my stomach like it always does when

I'm around someone or something that could cause my demise. I forced myself to put one foot in front of the other and before I knew it I was standing alongside the passenger-side door. "So, what did they want this time?" he continued.

"Who?" I wondered aloud.

"Don't play dumb with me," Kendrick hissed. He instantly became irritated with me. "I'm talking about the fucking cops. I saw you and your lawyer walk inside the station not too long ago."

"If you think your name came up, then you're wrong," I told him.

"What did y'all talk about?" Kendrick wanted to know.

I was taken aback by his question, so I hesitated for a moment. The first thought that came to my mind was that I'd be a damn fool if I told him the real reason why I was talking to the homicide detectives. But then again, I knew I couldn't lie to him. Kendrick has always been able to detect when someone was lying to him, so I was at a crossroads.

"Are you gonna stand there and look stupid or are you going to tell me what you and the cops were talking about?" he pressed the issue.

"They were asking me questions about my father's murder," I forced myself to say.

"What kind of questions?"

"They wanted to know when was the last time I talked to him and saw him."

Kendrick chuckled. "So they looking at you as a suspect, huh?"

"It's just a formality," I stated nonchalantly.

"But you and I both know who did it, right," Kendrick commented.

Taken aback once again by his question, I instantly had chills rolling down my spine. Kendrick was a creepy, dangerous guy. I knew I had to be careful with my words. "I don't understand what you're saying," I replied.

Kendrick sat up in his seat. "Kira, don't play with me. You know that I know you and Nick offed your pops. And I also know that you did it to get your man out of jail. When is he coming home? Today? Tomorrow?"

I stood there dumbfounded and at a loss for words. I honestly didn't know what to say. I felt like I had been caught red-handed. "Remember I know about everything that goes on in the streets of Miami," Kendrick said, to remind me of his influence.

"Whatcha trying to do, set me up?" I uttered from my mouth without even thinking about it first. The words just rolled off my tongue.

"Come here," Kendrick snapped. He reached his arm out toward me, grabbed ahold of my shirt, and pulled me towards the passenger-side door of the car. Before I knew it, Kendrick had jammed the barrel of a gun into my stomach. "Bitch, get smart with me again and I will put this lead in you so fast you ain't gonna know what hit you," he barked.

The impact of Kendrick pushing the gun in my side set off excruciating pain through my abdomen. I flinched and my knees started buckling. The only reason I didn't fall was because Kendrick held onto my shirt with a firm grip. "You don't think I would kill you right here, huh?" he continued, giving me a menacing look.

"Yes, I know you would."

"Well, if you know this then why are you talking shit?" he asked as he pressed the gun harder into my stomach.

"I'm sorry, I just got a lot on my mind right now." I said, while tears started falling from my eyes. I was becoming an emotional wreck and I was unsure as to how much more drama I could take in my life. Kendrick loosened his grip on my shirt when he saw me wiping tears off my face.

"I don't give a damn about your tears so clean that shit up," he growled. Like a newcomer in boot camp, I stood up straight and wiped my face clear of any tears. "All I brought you over here to say is, I know you whacked your pops so if I ever find out that you're helping the cops with any information concerning the judge and his wife, you're going down too. Are we clear?"

I continued to stand there and said absolutely nothing. I gave him a nod, because what could I possibly say? Everything he said was self-explanatory. If I ran my mouth off to the cops, he would make me pay for it.

Without saying another word to me, Kendrick looked at his driver and instructed him to drive away. I stood there watching Kendrick and his flunky leaving the service station. Boy, was I relieved to see him go. In a flash I rushed back to my car, hopped inside, and sped out of there as quickly as I could.

Instead of going in the direction of my apartment, I decided to take a drive out of Miami. Head up to West Palm Beach and turn back around. I knew this trip would give me some R & R. All the bullshit I had scrambling in my mind needed to go. I had no idea how I was going to release it, but I figured taking this long drive north would help me make sound decisions and get me out of this depressing state of mind. I prayed that it would work.

Chapter 15

Wearing a Brave Face

The one-hour drive to Never Never Land didn't help me like I thought it would. The fact that I murdered my father was going to take more than one drive in south Florida to put my mind at ease. To make matters worse, I had Detective Grimes and Kendrick breathing down my neck. From where I stood, that was 2 to 1. How in the hell could I compete? I didn't have the mental and physical stamina to go head-to-head with those guys. I could only take but so much. I knew one thing—if I didn't figure this shit out, I was probably about to have a nervous breakdown or worse.

Ten minutes after I turned my car around to head back down south to Miami, my cell phone started ringing. I pulled it out of my purse and honed in on the caller ID. The call was coming from the county jail, so I answered it because I knew it was Dylan calling. After I accepted his call, I waited for him to come on the line.

"Hello," he said after the recorded message ended.

"Hi, baby," I replied.

"Where are you?"

"Out taking a drive so I can clear my mind."

"Have you talked to my lawyer?"

"Not since the last time I talked to you. Why you ask?" I wanted to know.

"No reason," he said and paused. The phone line went silent. "I've got some good news," he continued.

"What is it?" I asked even though I suspected that his good news had something to do with him getting out of jail.

"My lawyer stopped by the jail a few minutes ago and told me that I'm going to court in two days, so get ready," he replied cheerfully.

"That's good, baby. I can't wait for you to come home."

"I can't wait either. I'm so fucking happy that this shit is almost over."

"So, will the charges be dismissed or what?"

"Yes, Mr. Berlinsky said he filed a motion to have my charges dismissed." Dylan spoke confidently.

"What time will your case be heard?"

"I believe he said ten o'clock. Be there at least thirty minutes ahead of time. You know court cases aren't ever called when they're supposed to be."

"Do you think they're going to release you the same day?"

"Of course they are. They wouldn't have any other reason to keep me."

"So, once they dismiss the charges, they can't come back and charge you again?"

"No baby, they won't be able to do it."

I let out a long sigh. "Good. Because I don't think I can be out here without you much longer."

"Have you talked to the cops again about your pop's death?" Dylan changed the subject.

"Yes, I spoke to them a few hours ago."

"Did they stop by the house again? Or did they ask you to come down to the station?"

"They asked me to come down to them."

"So what did they say?" he asked. It seemed like I was talking to Kendrick all over again. I mean, I just answered that exact same question a little over an hour ago and now I found myself answering it again. But was I going to give Dylan the same answer I gave Kendrick? Nope. I sure wasn't, especially since he was behind bars. All outgoing calls from the inmates were closely monitored.

"You know, the usual. Where was I the night my father was murdered? When was the last time I seen him? When was the last time I talked to him, questions like that."

"I hope those crackers don't think that I hired someone to kill him," Dylan sounded concerned.

"Who cares what they think? I'm so over them and the murders they are investigating."

"I feel the same way, but at the same time, I don't want to get caught up in something that I was never involved in. I see guys coming in this place every day that are in here for crimes they didn't commit. This jailhouse shit is serious. Locking up guys like me is big business. So cops are always on the prowl looking for their next victim which brings me to this, as soon as I get out of here, I want us to go on a trip away from here. Are you down for it?"

"Of course I am."

"Do you have any suggestions?" he asked me.

"Not really. But I'm sure you'll be able to come up with something."

"Have you had a chance to talk to my mother or sister yet?"

"I haven't spoken with them, but we've been texting back and forth."

"So you haven't gone back over there?"

"Yes, I went by there but there were no cars in the driveway so I left."

"You've been texting with my sister too?"

"Yes, I texted her and she finally texted me back and told me the reason why she hadn't gotten back with me was because she's been working double shifts at her job," I explained.

"What's up with Nick? Is he holding things down out there?"

"Yeah, he's doing his part so you don't have to worry about him."

"Have the cops left our apartment alone for good?"

"Yes, they have. We don't have to worry about them coming back for anything."

"Okay, all that sounds good but tell me, how are you feeling? Tell me what's on your mind."

"Trust me, there aren't enough minutes left on this call for me to tell you what's going on with me."

"When the call cuts off after the fifteen minutes is done, I'll call you right back," Dylan insisted. I could tell that he really wanted me to share my feelings and concerns with him. And believe me, I wanted to tell him that Kendrick jammed a gun in my stomach and threatened to kill me, but right now wasn't the time to do so. What I did do was tell him how much I loved him.

"Baby, I love you and I truly wish that you and I could leave Miami right now and never come back." I meant every word. I had thought relocating to Miami from Virginia would be a good thing, but in the end it had turned out to be my worst decision ever. It seems like trouble follows me everywhere I go.

"Just say the word and we will do that."

"You're acting like it's that easy."

"Because it is. You don't work at the car dealership anymore. And what I do I can do anywhere."

"What about our apartment? We just bought it."

"What about it? We can put it on the market and sell it."

"But what about your mother? We just can't leave her here with Bruce."

"We could convince her to come with us."

"Come on Dylan, you know your mother will not leave Bruce."

"If I tell her to leave 'em she will."

"Okay, well let's say that she agrees to leave Bruce, she's not going to leave the house your father bought her. That's just not going to happen. She cherishes that home. There's a lot of memories there."

"You just let me handle her," Dylan said confidently.

"No problem."

Dylan and I talked for another minute and a half. After the call time was up, he called me back. During this call, Dylan wanted to talk about the funeral arrangements I had planned for my father. When he first brought up the subject, something inside of me wanted to shut the whole conversation down, but when I thought about how the county jail records inmates' telephone calls, I decided it would be best if I played the part of mourning daughter, rather than an unconcerned bitch.

"So, how is everything coming along with your dad?"

"What do you mean?"

"Are you having a small funeral service? Huge? What?"

"Well, since I don't have any more family in the area, I plan to have a viewing so that the people my dad worked with can stop by and pay their respects. After that, I'm gonna have the funeral home take him where my mother is buried and lay him to rest beside her."

"Who is handling the funeral arrangements?"

"Dexter's."

"I've never heard of them. Are they good?"

"I don't know. You're acting like I plan funerals once a month," I replied sarcastically.

"Awww . . . baby, I'm sorry. You know I didn't mean it like that," Dylan started apologizing.

"It's okay, I know you didn't mean any harm."

"I'm glad because I love you so much and the last thing I ever want to do is stress you out. I mean, you already got a lot on your plate."

"Everything will get better soon enough," I assured him. I

only said it so he would stop apologizing. I knew he didn't mean any harm. Dylan was a great guy. And I knew he loved me. And considering what I did to my father—that's a testament as to how much I love Dylan.

At the end of our second phone call, he told me to text his sister Sonya and let her know that he'd be home in a few days. After I assured him that I'd do it, he told me that he loved me and that as soon as he got home he was going to take care of me. Take me away from all this murder and mayhem, with hopes that we would finally be able to live happily ever after.

Chapter 16

Hold Up! Wait A Minute!

The second after I got off the phone with Dylan, I texted his sister Sonya and told her the good news. Surprisingly, she texted me right back. *Let him know I miss him and I love him very much.*

Instead of texting her back, I dialed her cell phone number since I was driving. Her cell phone rang four times before the voicemail picked up. *You reached the right person, but the wrong time. Leave me a message at the sound of the beep.* BEEP!

"Sonya, this is Kira. I just text you and you text me back. What's going on? Hey listen, call me when you get a chance. Dylan is coming home in less than a week, and he really wants to see you and your mom. He also wants you to know that he loves you very much. Talk to you soon," I said, and I ended the voicemail message.

Immediately after I pressed the end button, I dialed Nick's cell phone number. "Hello," he said.

"Hey Nick, I got some good news," I stated.

"What's up?"

"I just got off the phone with Dylan. His lawyer got him a new court date and it's two days away."

"Will he be getting out?"

"Yes, that's the plan."

"Well, that's good. How does he feel about it?"

"He sounded pretty happy!"

"What about you? How do you feel knowing that he's getting ready to come home?"

"I can't really enjoy the idea of it because I'm trying to cope with my father's death."

"Have you called any of your relatives?" Nick asked.

"My dad had a second cousin, but he died a few years ago of a heart attack."

"What about your grandparents, are they still alive?"

"Nope. My father outlived my mother and his parents. I'm the last one left."

"Are you having a funeral for him?"

"Yes, sort of. Since he had a lot of friends downtown and at the courthouse, I'm gonna have a viewing at the funeral home. And when that's over, I'm gonna have him buried in the cemetery next to my mother."

"When is all of this going to take place?"

"In a couple of days."

"So, what's gonna happen to his house?"

"I don't know. I'm gonna eventually have to call his attorney so he can tell me what to do."

"I know this is kind of rough for you, but if you need anything just let me know."

"I really appreciate that, Nick."

"No problem, baby girl. Just keep your head up."

"I will," I assured him.

Before Nick and I ended our call, I heard a woman in the background making demands on Nick. I knew instantly that it was his new woman, Bianca. "I wish you would hurry up because I didn't come all the way over here to hear you talk on the damn phone," I heard her say.

Chapter 17

This Is Why I Love Him

The courtroom was packed from wall to wall with defendants, witnesses, snitches, the cops that arrested everyone and the lawyers that were there on payroll. It was becoming a media circus with the local news station setting up their camera equipment for a trial that was scheduled for 11:00 in the morning. Thank God Dylan's case was going to be called before that one.

I took a seat in the third row and waited patiently for Dylan's case to be called. His attorney, Mr. Berlinsky, was front and center, sitting at a table a few feet away from the judge. There were a couple more attorneys huddled around him carrying on a conversation. I wanted to let him know that I was in the courtroom, but only attorneys and courtroom officials were allowed in that area, so I remained seated. I figured he'd see me eventually.

After about 30 minutes, Mr. Berlinsky finally looked in my direction and headed toward me. He was sharp too. I know my fashion labels and from what I could see, so did he. I looked him over from head to toe and noticed that he had on a $2,000 custom-made suit, $1,000 Christian Louboutin loafers, and $500 Gucci cufflinks at his wrists. This guy was the real deal. "Got some good news for you," he started off.

I sighed heavily. "Thank God! After everything else that's been going on, I need some good news," I told him.

Mr. Berlinsky smiled as he moved in closer. "Well, I talked to the prosecutor, and he agreed to drop the charges because of your father's recent death. But I want you to let Dylan know that even though his charges will be dismissed today, the prosecutors will likely work behind the scenes in the hope of bringing another case against him. So tell him to be very careful."

"I will. And thank you so much, Mr. Berlinsky," I replied and then we shook hands.

"No problem. I'm here for you guys anytime," he assured me. But I knew what he really meant. As long as we got money, his phone line will always be open. The moment we go broke, he's going to put us on the block list.

After Mr. Berlinsky walked away from me, he headed back up to the front of the courtroom. A few minutes later, Dylan's case was called. I sat there and watched as the bailiff escorted Dylan into the courtroom. I smiled and winked my eye at him as soon as our eyes connected. He smiled back at me and I saw the relief on his face. He was finally getting his chance to become a free man.

"We're here today to address the motion for dismissal on case number 413570," the Caucasian judge announced as he read the case number from the documents placed in front of him.

"Yes, Your Honor, the state's only witness was killed unexpectedly a few days ago, and without this witness the state is unlikely to prevail in this case," Mr. Berlinsky stated.

The judge looked at the prosecutor and said, "Your entire case rested on this one witness who is now deceased?"

"Yes, Your Honor," the prosecutor replied. I couldn't see his face, but I could tell by the tone of his voice that he wasn't happy.

The judge looked down at the file in front of him and then

he looked back up. He turned his attention toward Mr. Berlinsky and Dylan, who was standing next to him. "I appreciate the hard work done by the state in investigating this case," the judge said. "However, when circumstances change after an indictment is issued and our judgment is that a case is no longer likely to be proven beyond a reasonable doubt, it is our duty to the defendant and to the court to dismiss that case. And in this case, the witness statement is inadmissible because it was made before the trial, and the witness cannot be cross-examined. This case is dismissed. The defendant is free to go." The judge continued and then I watched him as he signed three documents.

"Thank you, Your Honor," Mr. Berlinsky said.

"Yes, thank you, Your Honor," I heard Dylan say afterwards.

As soon as the bailiff grabbed ahold of Dylan's arm, Dylan turned around and gave me the biggest smile he could muster up. He was so happy. And so was I because my man was finally getting out of jail.

"Next case." I heard the judge say, which was my cue to exit the courtroom.

While I was leaving out of the courtroom, I realized there was a guy walking behind me. I turned around casually and what do you know, Detective Grimes was walking right on my heels. I instantly got a bad taste in my mouth, so I turned around to confront him. "What the hell do you want now?" I asked him sarcastically.

He gave me a smirk that irritated the crap out of me. "I'm just amazed at the lengths you'd go to to help your boyfriend get his case dismissed."

"All I did was get him the best attorney money could buy."

"Oh, you did more than that. And one day soon I'll be able to prove it," Detective Grimes said and then he turned around and walked off.

I was so shocked by his statement that I couldn't say another word. I just stood there in awe, wondering how I was going to stay a couple steps ahead of him. I mean, this guy really had it out for me. He made me feel like he hated my guts. I couldn't ever let him see me slipping because if I did, then I might as well kiss my freedom goodbye.

Chapter 18

It's Not Over!

I took a seat on one of the benches outside the courtroom after the run-in with Detective Grimes. I can't lie, this freaking guy had me on edge. The thought of him solving my father's murder made me feel sick to my stomach. I couldn't allow that to happen because that would send me to prison for the rest of my life. And I wasn't strong enough mentally to spend the rest of my life in prison. No way. My life would be spent out on the streets and I was going to make sure that that happened.

It took a few hours before Dylan was released. Mr. Berlinsky told me to meet him outside the gates near the visitor's entrance of the jail, so I did. And the moment I laid eyes on Dylan, I was instantly filled up with emotions and started crying. I raced toward him and jumped into his arms. I wrapped my legs around his waist and started kissing him passionately. "I love you so much!" I said after I kissed him four times.

"I love you too, baby. And now that I'm out of that joint, I'm gonna make sure I take good care of you. I'm handling everything from this point on, okay?" he said as he cupped my ass cheeks with both his hands.

"Okay," I said with a smile. And then it quickly dawned on me that I was acting like the late Whitney Houston acted when she jumped into Bobby Brown's arms after he was released from jail. I swear, it felt good to be in my man's arms again and I didn't want this moment to end.

After holding me for what felt like a little over one minute, he released me so I could stand on my feet. I stood there before him so I could get a good look at him. "You're so cute, but you need a hair cut baby," I commented in a joking manner.

He smiled. "Don't worry about it. I'm gonna get that taken care of right after you take me to see my mother."

"Well, let's go," I said.

"All right, then come on." Dylan replied. He grabbed my hand, and we walked hand in hand right up to the moment we reached my car. Like always, Dylan opened the car door for me and after I got inside he closed the door behind me.

Immediately after he got into the passenger seat, he closed the door and that's when I pulled off into the sunset. I think the fresh air was doing Dylan some good because for the first couple of minutes in the car, he rolled down the passenger-side window and laid his head against the headrest and closed his eyes. I knew he was in deep thought, so I didn't bother him.

———◆◆◆———

It was my idea to call his mother before we drove over to her place. Unfortunately for us, she didn't answer her cell phone. So then we called Sonya's cell phone number. She didn't answer her phone either. *You reached the right person, but the wrong time. Leave me a message at the sound of the beep.* BEEP! "Why the fuck aren't they answering their phones?" Dylan asked me. He sounded aggravated.

"Sonya texted me back the other day saying that she's working double shifts. And your mother is probably taking a nap or at church. She told me not too long ago that she's been volunteering at the daycare center the church just opened," I tried to reason.

"I'd rather see her doing anything than sitting at the house with that coward ass husband of hers," Dylan commented.

"Yeah, me too," I agreed. I watched Dylan dial Nick's cell phone number from my phone.

I heard his phone ring twice before he answered it. "You better be calling and telling me that they let my homeboy out!" Nick expressed with excitement.

"Come on man, you know they couldn't keep me forever!" Dylan bragged.

"Kira wasn't having it either way."

"Yeah, she held me down. So, where you at?" Dylan asked.

"I'm at Bianca's crib. Why, what's up?"

"Well, I'm on my way to my mom's house. But after I leave there, I wanna get with you so you can bring me up to speed about what's been going on with our investments."

"Oh yeah, let's do that. Meet me at my crib at eight o'clock tonight," I heard Nick say to Dylan.

"A'ight, see you then." Dylan replied.

<hr />

Dylan and I arrived at his mother's house in twenty-five minutes. Bruce's car was parked in the driveway, but Mrs. Daisy's car wasn't, so Dylan and I automatically assumed that she was spending her time at the church volunteering in the daycare center. But we wanted to make sure, so he got out of the car and knocked on the front door. Surprisingly, Bruce opened the door. He kept the glass storm door closed, though. I rolled down the car window so I could hear what they were saying. "Hey Bruce, what's up," Dylan started off.

"Nothing much, what can I do for you?" he wanted to know.

"I wanna see my mother. Where is she?"

"She's not here."

"I can see that. So tell me where I can find her."

"She's with your sister." he replied in an unconcerned tone.

"How long have they been gone?"

"I'm not really sure. Maybe two hours."

"Did she say where she and Sonya were going?"

"Nope," Bruce said coldly.

"Does she have her cell phone with her?"

"I'm sure she does."

"So, how is everything going with you and my mom?"

"Everything is going well."

"Well, I heard differently."

"Whatever you heard is a lie."

"Look, Bruce, I didn't come over here to get in an argument with you. I just wanna see my mother. That's it."

"Well, she's not here."

"Tell her to call me when she gets in. And if I don't hear from her by nightfall I'm coming back over here, okay?"

"You can do whatever you want to," Bruce said nonchalantly as they continued to stand in the doorway of the house, with the storm door between them. It seemed like everything Dylan said to him went in one ear and out the other.

This pissed Dylan off. He took one step closer to the storm door and said, "Come on Bruce, why you gotta be a smart ass? I'm trying to be civilized with you and you're trying to make this shit hard."

"Are you done?" Bruce asked sarcastically. From the look he gave Dylan, I knew shit was about to hit the fan so I hopped out of my car and rushed over to the front porch.

By the time I got within three feet of Dylan, he had taken another step toward the storm door. "Listen you fucking coward, 'cause I'm only gonna say this one more time. If my mother doesn't call me when she gets back, I'm gonna come over here and you and I are going to have a man-to-man conversation. Do you understand me?" Dylan roared. I could see the veins bulging on his neck. I grabbed him by the arm and tried to pull him back towards me.

"Dylan, come on baby, he's not worth it," I said.

"You better listen to your girlfriend," Bruce advised Dylan.

That set Dylan off. "What you just say to me, loser?" Dylan barked.

"I said, you better listen to your girlfriend," Bruce replied in a quiet, cynical manner.

I saw Dylan reach for the doorknob, so I grabbed his wrist and snatched it back. "Dylan, let's go right now," I pleaded. Dylan resisted a little. "Dylan, let's go and wait for your mom to call you."

Finally, after attempting four times to get Dylan to listen to me, he stopped resisting and allowed me to pull him away from the glass door. "You better have her call me before the night is over," Dylan warned Bruce as he exited the porch. Bruce didn't utter another word. Instead, he closed the front door and then I heard him lock it.

Immediately after we got back into my car, Dylan started cursing and talking about how badly he wanted to snatch the storm door off the hinges and beat Bruce's ass. "Kira, I swear I hate that fucking guy! And you have no idea how badly I want to kill that coward with my bare hands! I wanna snatch away his last breath," he roared as he sat forward in the passenger seat of my car.

I listened to him vent while I drove away from his mother's house. "Calm down, baby! He's a miserable old man. Trust me, he's gonna get what's coming to him," I said.

Chapter 19

Playtime Is Over

Dylan called his barber to get an appointment. Thankfully, the barber told him to come right over and he'd take care of him. Instead of going into the barbershop and waiting for Dylan to get his haircut, I elected to wait outside in the car. I needed to clear my head and sitting in a barbershop with a bunch of men running their mouths about women, the economy, and other nonsense wasn't how I wanted to spend the rest of my day. Trying to figure out my next move was what I needed to focus on. I couldn't say how long that was going to take, but I knew that the sooner I did it, the sooner I could stop being paranoid and looking over my shoulder every time I left my apartment. If it wasn't Kendrick or his boys watching me, it was that wanna-be super cop Detective Grimes. I wished everyone would just leave me alone already. Ugh!

While I was waiting for Dylan to get his haircut, I got a phone call from Eric, my contact guy down at Dexter's Funeral Home. I put the call on speaker after I answered it. "Hi Eric," I said. Eric didn't know it, but I was feeling uneasy with this conversation we were about to have.

"Hi Kira," he replied. "So, I'm calling you to let you know that your father's body is ready and that we're setting him out tonight in room number four for his viewing, which will start at nine a.m. tomorrow."

"Are we still having his funeral service at noon?" I asked him.

"Yes, we are. It's gonna start on time at the Roosevelt Cemetery."

"How long will the service be?" I continued to question him.

"Well since you aren't expecting a huge crowd, the service could take as little as thirty minutes, unless you want to stick around and watch the groundsmen lower his casket into the ground and cover it with dirt."

"No, I don't wanna see that. That will just tear me apart," I expressed. I've lied about a lot of things, but I wasn't lying about how I would be affected seeing my father's body lowered into the ground. He was being buried because I murdered him. There was no way I was going to allow guilt to ride me worse than it was already doing to me. I couldn't allow it to happen.

"Okay, that's fine. You're entitled to mourn your loved one the way you see fit. If you need anything else, call the office and either myself or my sister will take care of you," he assured me.

"Thank you so much," I replied and then we ended our call.

———◦◦◦———

Dylan's haircut appointment seemed like it took forever. When he walked back out to the car, I was resting my head against the headrest with my eyes closed. He startled me when he grabbed on the car door handle. I sat straight up, trying to focus my eyes on what had just happened. When I realized it was Dylan trying to get back into the car, I unlocked the car. "You just scared the shit out of me!" I told him.

"Baby, I'm sorry," he said while he was getting back into the car. After he closed the door, he kissed me on the cheek.

"It's okay," I said while I started up the ignition.

Dylan started massaging my right shoulder while I drove. "You got a lot of pressure going on in this area," he stated as he glanced over at me.

"I've got a lot of pressure in other places too," I said.

"Well, I'm gonna relieve you of all of it. From now on, I don't want you stressing out about anything. I'm home now so I'm gonna take care of everything," Dylan promised me. I didn't mention it to him, but I loved when he took charge of everything, leaving me with absolutely nothing to worry about. I loved that about him. Dylan was the best thing that ever happened to me. Hands down!

"I just got off the phone with a guy named Eric from the funeral home," I announced.

"What did he say?" Dylan wanted to know.

"He wanted me to know that my father's body was ready and that he'll be put in one of the rooms at the funeral home by morning. That way if anyone wants to stop by there to see him before the service starts at noon they'll be able to," I explained.

"How do you feel?" Dylan asked. He seemed really concerned.

"Baby, I don't know anymore."

"Have you thought about what's going to happen with your father's house?"

"No. I haven't thought about it."

"Do you have a relative somewhere that you can call to come down here to help you?" Dylan wanted to know.

"Not really. The ones I do have left are distant second and third cousins. And I haven't seen any of them since I went to a family reunion about fifteen years ago. I told you my family was small," I replied nonchalantly.

"Does he have a life insurance policy?"

"Yeah, he has one."

"You're the beneficiary, right?"

"I'm sure I am."

"You haven't called to check?"

"No, I haven't," I replied. His constant questions were irritating me.

"Well, who's paying for the funeral?"

"I am," I told him. "And don't worry, I'm using my own money." I wanted Dylan to be aware that I wasn't using any of his money, considering that my father was the reason he had been in jail.

"It's not about whose money you're using. I just want to make sure you call the insurance company because they aren't gonna reach out to you. They'd rather not pay the claim at all," he enlightened me.

"I'll call them after the funeral," I said. "Here, take my phone and call Sonya. See if she'll answer her phone now." I handed him my cell phone.

"I know what you're doing by telling me to call Sonya," he said as he took my cell phone from my hand. I didn't say another word. But he was right. He knew I wanted to get off the subject of my father's funeral. The only thing he didn't know was why I wanted to switch the subject. As badly as I wanted to tell him what I had done, this wasn't the time.

I watched him as he dialed his sister's cell phone number. But before the phone could ring, her voicemail message played. Dylan hadn't turned on the speakerphone but I could still hear it. *You reached the right person, but the wrong time. Leave me a message at the sound of the beep.* BEEP!

"Leave her a message," I whispered to him.

"Hey sis, you know who it is. Hit me and Kira up. We're trying to see you and Mama," Dylan said and then he disconnected the call.

"Wanna drive over to her house? If she's with your mother than they gotta be at her house, especially with all the shit Bruce has been putting her through," I suggested.

"What shit?" Dylan asked. He completely caught me off

guard. I had forgotten to tell him that Bruce had been physically abusing Mrs. Daisy.

"Baby, don't be mad at me—" I started off.

"What happened, Kira?" he asked me, already sounding angry. I hadn't opened my mouth to say anything yet.

"Sonya called me a week ago and told me that Bruce was at their house beating on your mother. Nick and I rode over there to check things out but Bruce wouldn't let us in the house. And when we called Sonya back to see where she was, she didn't answer her phone, so we left. I figured that one of them would call when they wanted me to come back over there."

"Are you fucking kidding me right now?!" Dylan roared. I could see his eyes turn blood shot red. "That fucking coward put his hands on my mother and you're just now telling me?"

"Baby, I'm sorry. But you were locked up when it happened. You were already dealing with the charges because of my dad so why stress you out even more? I mean, it's not like you could've done something about it. You're in jail for heaven's sake."

"It shouldn't have mattered where I was. Anything going on with my family, I wanna know about it. Simple as that. Now, turn this motherfucking car around and take me back to my mother's house. I'm gonna straighten that clown out once and for all."

"I'm not taking you back over there so you can catch another charge. Are you fucking crazy?"

"When it comes to my mother, do you think I care about getting another charge? I will kill that bitch ass coward with my bare hands," he roared.

"I know you will, that's why we're not going back there. We're going over to Sonya's house, so hopefully they are there. And if they are, then we can convince your mother to come back to the house with us. Deal?" I replied, trying to compromise with him.

"Nah, fuck that! Take me back to my mom's crib, Kira. I ain't gonna be able to live with myself if I don't deal with that motherfucker now!" Dylan said. He was rocking himself back and forth in the seat next to me. From the way things were looking, he wasn't going to let this thing go.

I pulled over to the side of the road and put the car in park. I turned and faced Dylan. "Baby, please listen to me," I began, "if we go to your mother's house right now, Bruce is going to call the cops on you, no questions asked. Now do you want to risk your freedom again? Look at it this way, you haven't been out of jail for twenty-four hours and you're making waves to go back inside. I can't let you do that. I need you out here with me." I gave him the sincerest expression I could muster up.

Dylan sat there for a moment. I could tell that he was fighting with trying to make a decision. So I sat there and waited for him to break his silence. "I'll tell you what, if you take me by my mom's house and I don't see her car parked outside then I won't go up to the front door," he proposed.

"Why go over there when she's probably at Sonya's place?" I countered.

"We just called Sonya and she didn't answer her phone. They may not even be there, which is why I'd rather ride back over to my mom's house. There's a possibility that she could be there by now," Dylan replied.

I sat there unable to say another word. Dylan was making it abundantly clear that he was going back to his mother's house and that was it. So I let him win this one and turned back around in my seat. I put my gearshift in drive, pulled back onto the road, and headed in the direction of Mrs. Daisy's house.

Chapter 20

What Did I Get Myself Into?

Dylan and I didn't say another word to each other the entire drive back to his mother's house. And even though I was quiet, I was praying silently the whole way there. I asked God to take control of his situation. I didn't want Dylan going back to jail. I needed him home with me. I couldn't continue to go head-to-head with Detective Grimes and Kendrick alone. I needed Dylan with me to ward off those evil ass men because sooner or later something more tragic than my dad dying is going to happen.

As soon as we turned onto Mrs. Daisy's street, Dylan sat up in the seat when we saw a car backing out of the driveway of his mother's house. It was dark outside, but we could see the shape of the back of the car and the taillights. "Hurry up, that looks like my mother's car," Dylan said in an urgent manner.

I pressed down on the accelerator and sped toward Mrs. Daisy's house. From what we could tell, it looked like we were finally going to see her. Optimism filled my entire body as I pulled up near the driveway. Before I could bring my car to a complete stop, Dylan hopped out of the passenger-side door. I watched him as he walked around the front of my car while I struggled to shift into park. I jumped out of the driver's seat a few seconds later.

"You are just the person I want to see," I heard Dylan say after I closed the driver's side door. And when I took a couple of steps towards the car, I realized it was Bruce's car and he was driving it. My heart dropped and all the optimism and excitement I had inside me quickly deflated. "Bruce, roll down the window so I can talk to you. As a matter of fact, get out of the car so we can have a man-to-man conversation," Dylan demanded as he pulled on the door handle a couple of times.

I couldn't hear a word Bruce was saying, but I saw his mouth moving. And I saw how carefully he was trying to back out of the driveway without rolling over Dylan or me. At one point, it seemed like he was warning Dylan to move out of the way before he rolled over top of us, but Dylan ignored him. So Bruce pressed down the accelerator and backed out of the driveway as quickly as he could without losing control. Dylan jumped into action and raced towards Bruce's car. "No, Dylan, don't . . ." I yelled, hoping he wouldn't do anything crazy like jump on the hood of the car or punch the windows out with his fists.

"You wanna put your hands on my mama? I am going to murder your ass tonight!" Dylan yelled as he scrambled to get as close to the car as quickly as possible. I scurried behind him hoping to stop him from doing something he would later regret. "Don't run you fucking coward!" Dylan huffed and started kicking the driver's side door with his feet.

"No Dylan, let him go," I yelled. Thankfully Bruce was able to put his car in drive and sped off before Dylan could get close enough to him to do any major damage.

I stood there trying to catch my breath while I watched Bruce drive away from the house. But that all went up in smoke when I noticed Dylan getting into the driver's seat of my car. "Where are you going?" I yelled while I ran back towards him.

"I'm going to get that motherfucker! Come on!" he roared.

I knew there was no way I could talk to him standing outside, so I hopped in the passenger seat and immediately started pleading with him. "Babe, what are you doing? You gotta stop before we both get arrested," I warned him.

"Fuck that! I'm gonna kill that motherfucker tonight," Dylan protested as he sped off behind Bruce's car.

"Dylan you can't do that. Remember we didn't come here for that. You promised me . . ." I pleaded with him while I was still facing him.

"He hit my mama, Kira. I can't let that go."

"I know Dylan. But getting him this way is only gonna put you back in jail. And I need you out here because . . ." I said and then I fell silent and started crying.

Dylan finally turned his attention toward me and slowed the car down. "Because what?" He asked me. I turned around in the seat and faced forward. "Pull the car over at that stop sign." I instructed him while I pointed to a stop sign half a block away. We were still in his mother's neighborhood so I felt like this would be a better place than any to break the news to him about my father's murder. The streets were quiet and from what I could see, there weren't any suspicious looking cars following us. I was surprised when Dylan pulled over and parked the car. I got out and he followed me. "Tell me what's going on."

I grabbed him and pulled him close to me. I leaned in so I could talk quietly in his ear. "I was the one who killed my father," I started off and when I tried tell him more, he grabbed both of my arms and pushed me back a little without letting me go.

"You did what?" he said, his words barely audible.

"I did it for you. I got Nick to take me to my dad's house, we drove him to an empty lot, I shot him and then I set the truck on fire."

"Who else knows about this?"

"Kendrick knows."

"How the fuck did he find out before me?" Dylan spat.

"I don't know. He saw me at the gas station two days ago and told me that he heard what I did. I tried to deny it but he didn't believe me."

"You know he's gonna hold that over your head, right?"

"Come on now, you know I'm not stupid."

"Well, don't worry about him. He's already on my hit list. I'm gonna make sure he never bothers you again."

Dylan pulled me back toward him and embraced me. He held me so tight, it felt like he was never gonna let me go. "Oh my God! Kira, I am so sorry you had to do that for me," he whispered back in my ear.

"I did it because I love you," I told him as I began to cry. When Dylan heard me sobbing, he held me even tighter.

"I love you too, baby. And I promise I will never let anyone separate us again," he promised me.

"Okay," I replied while the tears continued to fall from my eyes.

Dylan and I stood near the stop sign for a few more minutes and then we got back into the car. By now, Dylan was no longer concerned about hurting Bruce. After the news I had just given him, he was more concerned about me than anything else.

"Come on, let's go home. I think we should wait for Sonya or my mama to call us back," he said, and then we headed back to my car.

"All right," I agreed.

It felt good to finally tell Dylan my secret. I swear it felt like a burden was lifted from me. Now all we needed to concentrate on was getting past my father's funeral and getting Mrs. Daisy away from Bruce before he hurt her really bad and

Dylan ended up back in prison. I guess Dylan and I had some work to do.

When Dylan and I got back to our apartment we ate the Chinese food we'd picked up on the way home. Not long after we devoured our food Dylan carried me to our bedroom and fucked my brains out. I had to admit that the lovemaking session we had was long overdue.

While we were in bed trying to go to sleep Dylan wanted me to know that he planned to stop over at Sonya's house right after we left my father's funeral since she hadn't called us back. I told him that would be fine. At this point, whatever he felt was best for us, that was how things would be.

Chapter 21

Ashes to Ashes, Dust to Dust

I couldn't believe how tired I was until I woke up the next morning not wanting to get out of bed. That was the day I was burying my father, but I couldn't come to terms with the fact that I wasn't going to see him again. I felt like I was having a bad dream and that I was going to wake up from it at any given moment.

I was looking at myself in the vanity mirror connected to my bathroom sink. In just a little over a week, it looked like I had aged at least ten years. I had black circles around my eyes and my cheeks looked sunken in. Dylan walked up behind me and wrapped his arms around my waist. "Why aren't you dressed? You know the funeral starts in two hours," he reminded me.

"Don't worry, I'm gonna be ready on time," I told him.

Dylan kissed me on the back of my neck. "You know I love you, right," he whispered into my ear.

I looked at him in the mirror in front of us, "Yes I do," I replied and then I mustered up a smile.

He moved back from me and smacked me on the butt and said, "Well, hurry up and get ready. We've got a lot of stuff to do today."

I stood there for a few more minutes thinking about how I was going to react when I finally walked into the room where my father's body was being held. Was I going to continue to feel guilty or was I going to feel like my actions were justified? Either way, I knew I was going to have some strong feelings. I guess I was going to have to walk into that room to see which one was going to overpower the other.

Once I had gotten dressed in all-black funeral attire, I put on my dark shades, grabbed my purse and my car keys, and Dylan and I left the apartment. Instead of taking my car, we decided to take his. The valet attendants had his car in front of the building when we walked outside. "It's good to see you, sir," one of the valets said to Dylan.

"Yeah, it's been a while, huh?" Dylan commented as he handed the guy a twenty-dollar bill while another valet driver helped me into the passenger seat.

As soon as our doors were closed Dylan drove away from the curb. "Think they've been talking about us?" Dylan asked me.

"I'm sure they have," I replied while I stared out of the passenger-side window.

A few minutes later he sparked up another conversation. "Don't forget I said that we're gonna stop by Sonya's house after we leave the cemetery."

"Yes, I remember."

"Good. Hopefully, my mama is there too."

"I can't see why she wouldn't be," I said while I continued to stare out the window. But really, I couldn't care less what we did after the funeral. My main focus was getting through the funeral service. I only had enough energy inside of me for that chapter in my life. Nothing else meant anything to me right then.

It seemed like the closer we got to the funeral home, the heavier my anxiety weighed on me. I was a ball of nerves to put it mildly. And I couldn't tell how long I was going to feel this way. I prayed it would pass sooner rather than later.

Dylan and I arrived at the funeral home twenty minutes after we left our apartment. We walked hand in hand through the front entrance, where we were greeted by Eric and Gina Dexter. They were brother and sister—their parents had founded the funeral home. They were also appointed to handle the service for my father. "How was the drive here?" Eric asked us.

"It was fairly easy," Dylan told them.

"Great, I'm glad," Eric replied.

"So are you ready?" Gina asked with a sympathetic expression.

I wanted to answer her, but my mouth wouldn't open so I gave her a nod.

"Well, let me inform you that there are a few of your father's friends in the room viewing his body. We told them that as soon as you arrived we were going to start the service." Gina said.

Hearing her say that my father's friends were in the other room viewing his body kind of caught me off guard because he didn't have a lot of friends. Judge Mahoney and his wife were his closest friends and that was pretty much it. He did have a few former colleagues that he used to play golf with but that was over a decade ago. To label them friends seemed to be a little odd to me.

"How many people are actually in that room?" I finally was able to speak.

"There's a total of maybe five," she replied as she searched my face for a reaction. "Is everything alright?"

"Yes, everything is fine," I responded in a nonchalant manner. Truth be told, everything wasn't fine. I wanted to know who was in that room before I walked in there. I don't like surprises at all.

"Are you sure, baby? Because I can go and check things out while you stay right here," Dylan pressed the issue.

"No, I'm fine. Let's get this over with," I told him, and then I turned my attention towards Eric and Gina.

"Well, I guess you can follow us." Eric said and then he led the way to the room where my father's service was being held.

The knots in my stomach started twisting and turning as we walked toward the service area. At one point, it felt like my knees were going to buckle underneath me. Thankfully, Dylan held onto my arm the entire time.

Immediately after we entered into the room all eyes turned toward me. I recognized all five of the people sitting in chairs near my father's casket. Three of them were judges. One of them had denied Dylan bail at his hearing. The other two judges were really close to my father. The one woman in the bunch worked as my dad's courtroom clerk. Her name was Sandy Taylor. She was an attractive Hispanic woman who looked to be in her mid to late forties. I remembered how my dad used to talk about how loyal she was and how great her work performance was. So I walked over to her and thanked her for attending his farewell service. The three judges turned their heads. They sent me a clear message that they weren't interested in talking to me, so Dylan and I continued in the direction of a set of chairs to the left of the casket.

The fifth of my father's mourners was the prosecutor who had played a key role in getting Dylan's bail denied. I wanted to give him a piece of my mind, but I figured this wouldn't be a good time. We were supposed to be celebrating my father's home going and that's how it was going to be.

Once Dylan and I sat down, the chapel's minister came from the back room and the service started. "We are here on this day to seek comfort," he started off. "It would be unfair to say that our hearts aren't aching over this situation. But it would be fair to say that through it all, God is standing in our midst, and we should trust that He's going to minister to our hearts and give us the strength we need to move forward after this service is over and we lay this man to rest." He went on to brag about how nice my father was and how much the community loved him, which was a damn lie. He rambled on for another twenty-five minutes about how great my dad was and how he was in a better place. And he talked about how tomorrow isn't promised to us so we need to seek a personal relationship with God. The service was so emotional it felt like we were in church. And when he began the closing prayer to end the service it tore my heart in two. I wanted to run up to my father's casket and fall to my knees and pour my heart out to him. I wanted to tell him I was sorry. But I knew that wouldn't be a good idea. Every one of my father's former peers would have me arrested on the spot.

When the prayer was finally over, the minister thanked everyone for attending my father's service and then he dismissed us. Usually when friends attend a funeral, they would go out of their way to offer their condolences to the family, but not this handful of assholes. Every single one of those people left without saying goodbye, kiss my ass, or fuck you. They didn't even look in my direction after they marched out of the funeral home. They eyed me down when I first walked in the room. But now that the service was over, they wouldn't even acknowledge me. I said to hell with all of them. Rude motherfuckers!

───◦•◦───

The funeral officials loaded my father's casket into the hearse while Dylan and I got into his car. I assumed that the other judges, the prosecutor, and my father's former clerk were going to follow us to the cemetery but they drove off in the opposite direction when the hearse pulled away from the funeral home. Dylan noticed it too. "I guess it's just you and me going to the cemetery," he commented.

"I guess so," I replied.

"I can't believe the same prosecutor that tried to railroad my ass in court was there."

"I don't know why not. It wouldn't surprise me if all of them showed up to spy on us."

"If that's the case, we should've given them something to talk about."

"Nah, we acted like we were supposed to."

"How do you think the minister did at the service?"

"I guess he did alright. I mean, I really wasn't listening to him. I couldn't stop looking at my dad's casket," I said while I stared out the window.

Dylan massaged the back of my neck the entire drive to the cemetery and I have to admit that the touch of his hand made me feel better than I had before I walked into the funeral home over an hour ago. I knew Dylan loved me. I also believed that he was going to make things better. Crossing that hurdle would be somewhat complicated, but I figured once that part was over then I'd be home free.

When we arrived at the cemetery, the minister got out of the hearse and walked with Dylan and me to the burial site. A few minutes later, two of the funeral home officials rolled my father's casket from the hearse to the grave site. Dylan and I stood there and bowed our heads for another round of prayer. And when the minister closed the prayer with "In Jesus' name." I lifted my head up, blew a kiss at my father's casket, and then I turned around and walked back to Dylan's car. I swear I couldn't get out of the cemetery fast enough. Being centered around a bunch of dead bodies gave me an eerie feeling. Thank God Dylan was on the same page as me. I didn't have to tell him that I was ready to go, he already knew.

Chapter 22

No More Bad News!

As Dylan drove away from the cemetery, Nick called Dylan to confirm a meeting they were having later. "Kira and I just left the funeral and now we're on our way to Sonya's house. As soon as I drop Kira back off to our apartment, I'll head over there," I heard Dylan say. After Nick agreed to the time of the meeting, they ended their call.

Upon entering the Coral Gables neighborhood where Sonya lived, Dylan stated that he and his sister were going to find a way to get Bruce out of their mother's house. "Do you think my attorney could help me with that?" he asked me as we cruised through the neighborhood.

"I don't see why not," I stated without looking at him.

"Well I hope so, because he's gotta go. I can't have anyone putting their hands on anyone I love. That's unacceptable." Dylan paused and then a moment later said, "Hey wait, I don't see Sonya's car."

I turned my attention toward a row of townhouses and noticed that Dylan was right. Sonya's car wasn't parked in her driveway. "Think she might be at work?" Dylan asked me.

"She could be," I replied.

"Do you have the number at her job?" he asked me as he pulled into a parking space directly in front of her townhouse.

"I think so," I told him and then I grabbed my phone from my purse. I searched my contact list and found a phone number for Sonya's job. I dialed it and waited for someone to answer. I heard a woman say, *Thank you for calling Assisted Living, how can I help you*, and I turned on the speakerphone so Dylan could hear the conversation.

"Hi, my name is Kira and I'm looking for Sonya Callender-Morris. I'm her sister-in-law and I've been trying to contact her for the last couple of days with virtually no luck. I was wondering if I could speak with her for a minute or so if she's available?"

"I'm sorry, ma'am, but Sonya hasn't been to work in over a week now. We've been trying to contact her ourselves," The woman said.

"What do you mean she hasn't been to work?" Dylan blurted out.

"Ma'am, are you sure?" I asked. I instantly became sick to my stomach. I couldn't fathom Sonya missing work. Was she alright?

"Yes, I'm positive. I've sent one of my staff members over to her place after the third day and they left a note on her door letting her know that we were worried about her and that she needed to give us a call."

"Oh my God! This can't be," I said while I stared into Dylan's eyes, at the same time trying to figure out where in the hell Sonya could be.

"My name is Amy Glass. When you get a chance to speak with her, please let her know that she needs to give us a call."

"I most certainly will," I assured the woman and then I ended the call.

"What the fuck is going on?" Dylan cursed. I could see the veins in his temple flaring up.

"Do you think this has something to do with Bruce? I mean, what if he has her and your mother tied up in the basement of that house?" I asked suspiciously.

"I'm telling you right now, if that motherfucker touched a hair on my mother or sister's head, no one is gonna stop me from killing him."

"Baby, let's not think the worst. There's gotta be a good explanation why Sonya hasn't been to work. So let's start here."

"What do you mean?" he asked.

"You have a spare key to her place, right?"

"Yeah,"

"Well, let's go inside and check things out. Who knows, maybe she left town without telling us."

Without saying another word Dylan exited the car. I followed him. After Dylan figured out which key on his key ring belonged to Sonya, he unlocked the front door and we let ourselves in. A stale smell hit me in the nose instantly as I made my way down the hallway. It wasn't an odor indicating that there was a corpse in the house, so I was fine with it.

From the looks of things, nothing seemed out of place. The kitchen was spotless and so was the living room. "She keeps a pretty clean house," I pointed out as I scanned both rooms. Dylan didn't comment. Instead, he stepped away from me and headed in the direction of Sonya's bedroom. I followed suit.

As soon as we entered Sonya's bedroom we noticed that her bed hadn't been made. But still, nothing was out of place in a way that suggested something had happened to her. "Check her closet," Dylan instructed me while he searched underneath her bed.

"I'm on it," I told him and marched over to her walk-in closet. When I opened the door, I noticed that her favorite suitcase that she used every time she left town was tucked away next to a box where she kept her hats. This wasn't a good sign. "Baby, I don't think Sonya left town."

Dylan got to his feet. "What do you mean?" He walked toward me.

I grabbed her favorite suitcase and pulled it out of the closet. "She never leaves town without this suitcase. It's her favorite. I think we should call the police," I said.

"Wait, let me call her one more time first." Dylan pulled his cell phone out and dialed Sonya's number. Once again the voicemail played before the phone could ring. *You reached the right person, but the wrong time. Leave me a message at the sound of the beep.* BEEP!

Dylan hung up and dialed Sonya again. The voicemail message played again. *You reached the right person, but the wrong time. Leave me a message at the sound of the beep.* BEEP!

"I'm calling the cops," I announced. I took my cell phone out of my purse and dialed 911. "911, what's your emergency?" A female dispatcher asked.

"Umm, I want to report a missing person. Her name is Sonya Callender-Morris and we believe that she's been missing for over a week."

"What makes you think she's been missing for over a week?"

"Because that's the last time we spoke to her. And the people at her job say that she hasn't been to work for more than a week," I explained.

"How old is she?" the operator asked.

"She's thirty."

"Is she married or single?"

"She's married. But her husband is on deployment in Afghanistan."

"Have you been to her house?"

"Her brother and I are here now. We have a spare key to her home."

"What's the address to that residence?"

"It's 301 Madeira Avenue."

"Okay, well sit tight. I just dispatched a unit so they should be there soon."

"Thank you," I said and then I ended the call. "Come on, let's wait for them outside." I walked towards the front door, and Dylan followed me without saying anything.

Chapter 23

Missing Persons

Two white male police officers showed up at Sonya's house about ten minutes later. Dylan and I met them on the front porch. The officers introduced themselves as Officer Towson and Officer Vass and they started asking Dylan and I a long list of questions about Sonya.

"You say she's been missing for over a week?" Officer Vass asked.

"Yes," I replied.

"Do you think she could've left town?" he continued to question me.

"No, she's very close with us. She would tell us if she had to leave. Not only that, she loves her job and we just found out a few minutes ago that she hasn't been there in over a week."

"Have you tried contacting her on her cell phone?"

Dylan interjected, "We've been trying to call her for the last couple of days, but her phone goes straight to voicemail. We've also been trying to get in touch with my mother. We think they might be together."

"Does your mother live here too?" Officer Towson asked.

"No, she lives across town with her abusive husband. He's been keeping us from seeing my mother too."

"Are you saying that your mother is missing too?" the same officer asked.

"I'm not sure. My fiancée and I have been over there a few times, but her husband keeps telling us that she's not there, that she's with my sister. I think he's holding them hostage in my mom's house," Dylan told him.

"Don't say that, Dylan, you don't know that for sure," I blurted out.

"What's your mother's address?" Officer Vass asked.

"I don't know it, but I can show you where it is," Dylan offered.

"Okay. Let us take a look around your sister's place and then we'll follow you over to your mother's house," Officer Vass replied.

"All right, well we'll wait out here until you're done," I told him.

"Good. We will be right back," Officer Vass said and then they went into Sonya's house.

After they disappeared into the house I turned towards Dylan. "Why would you tell them that Bruce may be holding them hostage?"

"Where else can they be, Kira? They aren't here. And didn't he tell us that they were together?"

"Yes, but—" I began to argue, but Dylan cut me off in midsentence.

"But nothing . . . He knows where they are and if he doesn't tell me, I'm gonna kill him."

"You're gonna kill who?" Officer Towson asked when he reemerged from Sonya's house.

"I'm talking about my mother's husband," Dylan repeated himself without hesitating.

"He doesn't really mean that. He's just venting because he's frustrated," I interjected.

Officer Towson didn't say another word. He did give Dylan a bizarre look.

"So, are y'all ready to head over to his mother's house?" I continued, trying to lighten the mood.

"As soon as my partner comes out, we'll do that," the officer replied.

"Well, we're gonna wait in the car until he does," Dylan said.

"Wouldn't it be a good idea to lock the front door after my partner comes out?" Officer Towson asked.

"He can lock it from the inside and close the door," Dylan said.

"I'll make sure he does that," Officer Towson assured us.

Dylan and I climbed back into his car and waited for the other officer to come out of Sonya's house. He resurfaced a few minutes later. Officer Towson instructed Officer Vass to lock the front door from the inside and then they both got into their squad car.

Dylan backed out of the parking space we were in and then we headed in the direction of his mother's house. The ride was smooth but the thought of two cops following us seemed kind of weird. "Think they ran your license plate?" I asked.

"I could care less. Finding my sister is way more important than trying to find out who I am," he replied.

"If Bruce is at the house, do you think he's going to let us in?" I wondered aloud.

"That's my father's house so he better let me in," Dylan hissed.

"Baby, listen, I know you wanna tear that asshole in half, but you gotta be careful about how you act and what you say around the cops. You don't want them hauling your ass back downtown," I warned him.

"I don't give a damn about that!" he huffed.

I pinched his thigh. "Dylan, you promised me." I reminded him about not leaving me alone out on the streets again while he went back to jail.

"Well, just keep that moron away from me," Dylan urged.

"Don't worry, I will," I assured him.

———————

Dylan pulled his car curbside in front of his mother's house, while the officers parked their vehicle directly behind Bruce's car. Once again, there was no sign of Mrs. Daisy's car, which worried me.

"Do you want us to go up to the house with you?" Dylan yelled from the car window.

"Actually we'd prefer if you'd stay in the car," Officer Vass replied.

Ignoring the officer's suggestion, Dylan got out of the car and I followed him. "What about if I stand here on the side-walk?" Dylan countered.

"That's fine. But stay back. Officer Towson and I will han-dle things from here."

I stood alongside Dylan while both officers walked up to his mother's house. My heart raced at the speed of lightning. I was having so many different thoughts run through my head I couldn't think clearly. I'd been to this house with Nick and Dylan and we'd never been able to get Bruce to open that front door. Hopefully, the officers would intimidate him enough that he would either let us see Mrs. Daisy or tell us exactly where she and Sonya were. "Think he's gonna answer the door?" I asked Dylan while Officer Vass rang the doorbell.

"I guess we'll see," Dylan replied.

Officer Vass rang the doorbell and also knocked on the door. I wasn't counting but it seemed like he knocked and rang the doorbell almost ten times. "Looks like that bastard ain't opening the door," Dylan stated.

I sighed. "I guess you're right." I saw both officers turn around to exit the porch. When they reached the driveway, Bruce opened the front door. "Hey look, he opened the door," I yelled, trying to get the officers' attention.

"Look, he's standing in the door," Dylan yelled.

Both officers turned around and saw Bruce standing on the other side of the glass storm door, so they walked back to the porch to approach him. "Think he's gonna let them in?" I asked Dylan.

"I don't even wanna think about it."

"I wonder what they're saying to him."

"Yeah, and I'm wondering what kind of lies he's telling them," Dylan said.

"We'll soon find out," I said while I watched Bruce's body language on the other side of the glass door. He looked like he was playing cool, like he was in control. That wasn't a good sign for Dylan and me. The goal was to get the officers to scare him, not let him control the situation.

"Wait, is he coming outside?" Dylan wondered aloud.

"It looks that way," I answered while I watched Bruce push the storm door open. Seconds later he stepped onto the porch and closed the storm door behind him.

We couldn't hear anything he was saying, and that frustrated Dylan. "What the fuck is going on? What are they saying to him?" Dylan started getting impatient.

"Baby, calm down. They got him to step outside so let's wait and see what happens," I managed to say.

"I understand all of that, but they are taking too damn long. I need to see my mother and my sister." He spat.

Before I could comment, Officer Towson left Officer Vass on the porch with Bruce while he strolled toward Dylan and me. The moment he was within arm's reach Dylan asked his first question. "Does he know where my sister is?"

"He says he doesn't know. He says he hasn't seen her in a couple of days," Officer Towson replied.

"Sir, he is lying," I interjected.

"Well, did he tell you where my mother is? Because it seems like every time we come by here, he says that she either just left or she's asleep."

"Sorry to say, he just gave us that same excuse," the officer said.

"Listen officer, he's gonna have to give me a better answer than that. And I'm not leaving here until he does. As a matter of fact, tell him to let us in the house so we can check things out for ourselves," Dylan suggested.

"I can only ask him because that is his property."

"That is not his house. That's my mother's house. My father put her in that house," Dylan snapped.

I grabbed Dylan by the arm. "Baby, please calm down."

Dylan started yelling. "Nah, fuck that! Bruce you think we're stupid. Whatcha put your hands on my mama again and now you're trying to hide her so we can't see the bruises? And tell me where my sister is. Whatcha got her tied up in the basement or something? 'Cause she ain't been to work in a week."

"Sir, I'm gonna have to ask you to leave if you don't calm down and control yourself," Officer Towson warned Dylan.

"Dylan, please stop," I began to beg him, but my words fell on deaf ears. Dylan snatched his arm away from me and made a run for the front porch. He sprinted across the lawn and jumped on the porch, missing all three steps that led up to the front door. Luckily for Bruce, Officer Vass saw him coming and ushered Bruce back into the house. "Where the fuck is my mother and my sister, Bruce? Tell me where they at?" Dylan roared.

I finally made my way up to the porch, hoping I could help defuse the situation before the officers hauled Dylan off to jail. "Sir, we're gonna ask you to leave off the property. If you don't go, we're going to have to arrest you," Officer Towson threatened him.

I reached for the back of Dylan's shirt and tugged on it. "Baby, come on, let's go."

"Bruce, answer my question. Where's my sister and my mama!" Dylan panted.

"You better listen to her," Officer Towson told him.

Dylan turned toward me and started making his way back down off the porch. But before he stepped off the last step, he looked back at the door while Bruce was standing there and said, "If I find out that you did something to my family, I'm telling you right now you better leave town ASAP."

"Come on baby," I said once again, tugging on his shirt with a little more force. Thank God, this time he listened.

After Dylan and I climbed back into his car, both officers and Bruce kept their eyes on us as Dylan drove away. "Did you see how Bruce manipulated that whole situation?" Dylan roared.

"He sure did, because the main reason we had them follow us over there was so that he could tell us where Sonya was since he said she was with my mama just yesterday. Now all of a sudden he doesn't know shit."

"So what are we going to do now?" I wanted to know.

"I'm gonna get you to drop me off at Nick's spot. I'll get him to bring me home later."

"What's the plan?"

"The less you know, the better off you'll be . . ." Dylan trailed off and he fell silent.

"Dylan please don't go back over to your mother's house."

"Listen, I don't care what no one says, I'm gonna find my mother and sister tonight." I refused to dignify that statement with a comment. Right now, Dylan was in his feelings, so I left well enough alone.

It took Dylan about twenty minutes to get to Nick's place. He pulled up to the apartment building, kissed me on the mouth, and then he hopped out of the car. I wanted to say something to him about the way he was carrying on, but I didn't. Instead, I crawled over into the driver's seat, put the car in drive, and sped off.

———

I don't know how I got home without having a nervous breakdown, but I thank God that I didn't. When I entered the parking garage, I couldn't hold the tears back. After I parked Dylan's car in the designated parking space, I sat there in the driver's seat and starting sobbing uncontrollably. I couldn't stop thinking about how things would be different if I hadn't gotten involved with Kendrick. My father wouldn't be dead, my former co-worker Nancy wouldn't be dead, the Mahoneys wouldn't be dead. And who knows, maybe Kendrick had something to do with Sonya's disappearance. It was too much of a coincidence that no one had seen Sonya in over a week. But then when I thought about getting that text message from her a few days before, I couldn't help but wonder if that was really her. Whatever the case, she was gone and we needed to find her.

Chapter 24

We're Fucked!

I sat in Dylan's car and sobbed for almost an hour. I finally willed my way out of the car after one of my neighbors saw me crying and offered to walk me to my apartment. I accepted his hospitality and allowed him to do just that.

As soon as I entered my apartment, I drank a glass of water and then I lay down on the living room sofa. I couldn't tell you how long I slept, but when I woke up and saw that it was ten o'clock at night, I became worried because there was no evidence that Dylan had come home while I was asleep. When I tried to get him on the phone, he didn't answer. In my mind, this wasn't good. The threats he'd made about killing Bruce kept playing over and over in my head. I just hoped that he hadn't gone through with it.

After ten minutes, I picked up my cell phone and tried to call him again. But I got no answer. Then I dialed Nick's number because I knew they were together. Nick didn't answer his phone either. His voicemail picked up on the second ring. "Fuck!" I screeched and then I threw my phone down on the sofa.

I knew I wasn't going to be able to sit in the apartment and wait for Dylan to come home, so I grabbed my purse and my car keys and headed toward the front door. I said a silent prayer, "God please be with me," and then I opened the front door.

"Fuck!" I blurted out, after opening my door and seeing Detective Grimes standing in the entryway with the same police officers who had followed Dylan and me to Mrs. Daisy's house earlier. I knew something was about to go awfully wrong. I braced myself for the inevitable.

"Did we scare you?" Detective Grimes asked me while his partner and the two officers stood alongside him.

I looked at his partner and the other two officers, and then I looked back at him. "What do y'all want now? Aren't you tired of harassing me?" I asked him. I wasn't in the mood to deal with him and his shenanigans. I had other pressing matters on my mind that needed to be dealt with.

"We came to see if Dylan was home," he said.

"What do you want with him? Wasn't his case dismissed a couple days ago?" I spat.

Before Detective Grimes could answer, Dylan came strolling down the hallway. Detective Brady saw him first. He nudged Detective Grimes to get his attention. "Mr. Callender, your timing is impeccable," Detective Grimes commented.

When I saw Dylan's face, I knew he wasn't too happy to see all these cops standing at our front door. "Man, what the fuck y'all want now?" He roared.

"We just need to ask you a few questions," Detective Brady said.

"I see you got the two officers with you that kept me from going upside my mother's husband's head earlier today," Dylan said. By this time, Dylan was standing next to me in the doorway like he was ready to go toe to toe with these cops.

"Can we come in?" Detective Grimes asked boldly.

"Fuck nah! Are y'all motherfuckers crazy?" Dylan snapped.

"Look, just tell us why you came here," I interjected.

Detective Grimes looked at me and then he turned to face

Dylan. "We came by to let you know that we found your mother's and sister's bodies."

Hearing the words, *we found your mother's and sister's bodies* hit me in the chest like a ton of bricks. It hit Dylan even harder. I grabbed him by the arm and instantly felt him stiffening up. "What do you mean when you say bodies?" Dylan needed clarity.

"They're both deceased," Officer Towson spoke up. He was the same officer from earlier that talked to us while his partner Officer Vass talked to Bruce on the front porch.

"There's got to be some kind of mistake. There's no way that my mama and my sister is dead." Dylan replied.

"How do you know that it's them?" I asked.

"They both had their identification cards on their persons," Detective Grimes stated.

"Where did you find their bodies?" Dylan wanted to know, his voice started cracking.

"In a storage unit that your mother's husband rented two weeks ago. And based on the level of the decomposition, that was also around the time they were murdered," Detective Grimes replied.

"Oh my God!" I said, feeling completely horrified.

"So, that motherfucker really killed my family?" Dylan roared as he broke away from my grip.

"We can't answer that question right now. But we are investigating all of the evidence fully," Detective Brady explained.

"Come on now with that bullshit! You know that asshole murdered my family." Dylan huffed. "And where is he anyway? Did y'all arrest him yet?" Dylan's questions continued. He stood toe to toe with Detective Grimes and the other cops. Dylan's posture was stern so they knew that he was serious.

"I'm sorry, but he's dead too," Officer Vass finally spoke.

"What the fuck do you mean he's dead?" Dylan challenged Officer Vass.

"After we found your mother and your sister, we went by

the house to execute a search warrant and immediately after we entered the home, we found him lying on the floor of your mother's bedroom in a pool of his own blood. It appears that he shot himself in the head, but we don't know that for sure. The gun was found a few feet away from his body," Grimes continued, as he looked at Dylan and me.

"Why the hell are you looking at us like that?"

"Because his death has not been ruled a suicide. I have two officers here that heard you threaten to kill your mother's husband several times," Grimes said in a matter-of-fact kind of way.

"Oh so now y'all wanna pin his death on me?" Dylan replied sarcastically.

"Only time will tell. But right now, we're gonna need both of you to come down to the station so we can get a formal statement from you."

"I'm calling my lawyer before I go anywhere with you," I told them.

"By all means," Detective Grimes replied as he stood there in the doorway.

I walked away from my front door to retrieve my purse and my cell phone. It was close to eleven at night and these assholes wanted to fuck with Dylan and me. I couldn't believe that Dylan and I were faced with yet another fucking murder investigation. When was all this shit going to end?

If you enjoyed *Wifey's Next Come Up*,
you will love Kiki Swinson's newest thriller
Burning Season!

Prologue

When Things Went Left

I couldn't believe that I was sitting in the bank manager's office talking to federal agents about a check I was trying to deposit into my account, along with money I already had sitting in there. Could I really get locked up for the rest of my life? To hear the words "will spend the rest of your life in federal prison" evoked a different kind of reaction inside me. I'd seen Court TV and the reactions of men and women after they got sentenced to lengthy prison terms. I'd also heard so many horror stories about doing prison time with other inmates that are dangerous and will kill you for a fucking honey bun, or to prove a point, and that wasn't my idea of how I wanted to live out the rest of my life. I wanted to have kids and watch them grow up, go off to college, and have families of their own.

Sitting here in this chair, surrounded by federal officers, was not the ticket. All I had to do was tell them that Alonzo gave me the check, but then where would that leave him? I'd be ratting my brother out and that went against everything that I believed in. I was taught as a child that family stuck together. Never let anyone come between us. Our father embedded that in our family's heads. Zo lived by those same values. So I refused to let any agent come between that.

"Excuse me, Agents. But am I under arrest?"

Both agents looked at one another. And then they turned their attention toward me. "No, you're not," the female federal agent replied.

I stood up and walked toward the door of the bank manager's office.

"You know that if you walk out of here, there's no coming back," the female federal agent commented.

"Say no more," I told her, and then exited the office. The agents watched as the door closed shut.

Chapter 1

Alayna

I was on the phone talking when Levi entered our bedroom. "I'm gonna call you back," I told the caller, and then ended the call. This pissed Levi off.

"Who was that? And why did you end the call when I walked into the bedroom?"

"I didn't end the call because you walked in. I was going to end it anyway."

"It must've been your side piece."

"What side piece? Trust me, you're all the man I can handle at once," I said, trying to assure him. But he wasn't buying it. Levi knows that things have changed in our marriage. We have sex less and I don't spend time with him like I used to. And this bothered him. I mean, if the shoe was on the other foot, it would bother me too.

"Come on, let's get out of here. I've gotta get to work," he mentioned, and left the bedroom.

He was sitting inside my car when I exited the house. He and I had been carpooling for the past week because his 2017 Dodge Charger was in the shop getting a new transmission. My 2021 Jeep Wrangler was his source of transportation for the moment and he hated it, especially when he had to drop me off at work in front of Tim and my brother, Alonzo.

All eyes were on us when we pulled up in the parking lot. Tim, Alonzo, Jesse, and the volunteer Paul were sitting on the picnic table that the firemen use to congregate and shoot the breeze when we're not cleaning the fire station or one of the trucks.

As soon as Levi stopped the Jeep, I gave him a quick peck on the lips and then climbed out of it. "What kind of kiss was that?"

"What do you mean 'what kind of kiss was that?' It was a kiss."

"I see what you're doing?"

"What are you talking about?" I asked while standing next to the passenger-side door.

"You tried to hurry up and kiss me so your boyfriend wouldn't see you," Levi said as he watched my brother, Alonzo, approach my Jeep.

"What's going on, family?" Alonzo asked after he came within arm's distance of us.

"Everything is all good." Levi spoke first.

———◆◆———

Alonzo turned his attention towards me. "Ready to work?" Alonzo asked me.

"As always," I replied.

"Do you know what you're trying to cook tonight?" Alonzo reminded me.

"Oh, yeah. I forgot."

"We're all gonna pile into the truck and head to the store in about thirty minutes. So put a list together," he encouraged me.

"Will do," I said, and walked away from the Jeep.

"You ain't gonna say goodbye to your man?" Alonzo blurted out.

"I kissed him earlier," I said without looking back.

"She's trying to hurry up and get over there to her boy-friend," Levi commented.

Alonzo burst into laughter. "Who? Tim?"

"Yeah, her sugar daddy."

I pretended not to hear him say that.

"Oh, nah, ain't nothing going on with those two," I heard my brother say.

"Alonzo, don't blow smoke up my ass. I know what I see."

"Well, if you think you see something, then I'm not gonna argue with you."

"I appreciate it," Levi said, and then sped off.

Me and Tim watched as Levi sped away in my Jeep.

"Looks like someone is upset," Tim commented.

"He's just being a jerk," I replied.

"He thinks you two are having a fling," Alonzo mentioned.

Tim and I both looked at one another and then we looked at Alonzo.

"What gave him that impression?" Tim asked Alonzo.

"He didn't say," Alonzo answered.

"I told him that he needs to stop being so insecure," I added.

"What made him suspect something was going on between you guys in the first place?"

"He complains about Tim texting me too much."

"He's your boss," Alonzo interjected.

"I told him that," I said.

"Did you tell Alonzo that he called me the night before, asking where you were?" Tim chimed in.

"No," I replied.

"While you were here at work?" Alonzo asked, wanting clarity.

"Yeah. I had just washed the dishes in the kitchen."

"And I was helping him."

"Where was I?" Alonzo wanted to know.

"I think you and Jesse was outside cleaning up the truck by then," I answered.

"I wonder why he didn't call me?" Alonzo asked us.

"He's still salty about how you screamed at him during the NBA Finals and never paid the bet you owed him," I explained.

"No way. He still thinks I owe him?"

"Yep. He bet on the Bucks winning. And your money was on the Phoenix Suns."

"Yeah, but the Bucks was supposed to beat the Suns by ten points. But they only got them by seven."

I chuckled. "He said that was bullshit and that you threw that ten point–game clause in there when the game was almost over."

Tim chuckled. "That sounds like you, Alonzo."

"No. I added that during halftime."

"Alonzo, just pay him the money," I insisted.

"I don't even remember how much the bet was."

"One hundred dollars," I reminded him.

"One hundred dollars?" Tim interjected. "Oh, Levi can forget it. This cheap motherfucker here isn't going to give anyone one hundred dollars."

"Yeah, I don't remember it being that much," Alonzo added.

I let out a long sigh. "Alonzo, just give Levi the money. He won it fair and square."

"I'm not giving him one hundred bucks. Maybe twenty." Alonzo flat out refused.

"Why don't you give him fifty instead?" Tim suggested.

"Yeah, that would be a nice gesture. Meet him in the middle," I agreed.

"I'm not giving up one hundred or fifty. Twenty-five dollars is my final offer."

I threw my hands up in the air. "Getting money out of Alonzo is like pulling teeth," I commented, and then walked off and headed into the fire station. Jesse and Paul followed me.

"Don't get mad because I know how to hold on to my money!" he yelled behind me.

I ignored him and continued into the building, leaving them two out there alone. Hanging out at the fire station was my passion. I lived for this place, and it didn't hurt that I had a little love thing going on with Tim while I was here. This would kill Levi. But I figured what he didn't know wouldn't hurt him.

Chapter 2

Alonzo

"Remind me never to bet against you on anything," Tim commented, and then he chuckled.

Before I could respond, my cellular phone started ringing, so I retrieved the phone from his side pocket and looked at the caller ID. It was my fiancée, Pricilla Gates. I met Pricilla at a sports bar. I was there with a couple of high school buddies watching the play-offs and introduced myself. We talked and hit it off, and fast-forward three years later, we're still together. Just seven months ago, I proposed to her and she said yes, so we're now planning a wedding. Hopefully, kids will follow.

"Hey, future Mrs. Riddick, how can I help you?" I started off the conversation, and put her on speakerphone.

"I'm good, baby. I was calling to remind you that we have a cake tasting on Friday. That's the day you get off, so don't take on an extra day there at the station."

I started laughing.

"Don't laugh. I'm serious. You tried that stunt before and I had to reschedule."

"Pricilla, I'm gonna make sure he makes that appointment," Tim interjected.

"Is that Tim?"

"Yes, it's me."

"How are you?"

"I'm great, and you?"

"I'm good. And, yes, please make sure he doesn't try to stay there after his shift is over Friday morning."

"I will, and you have my word," Tim assured her.

"Thank you, Tim. Okay, baby, you there?"

"Yes, I'm here."

"I'm gonna go now. I love you."

"I love you too," I told her, and then ended the call.

"Sounds like you're dragging your feet. You're not having second thoughts, are you?"

"Oh, no, I've just been busy, trying to get this money. I told her to go and do the cake tasting with her mother and her sister. But, no, she wants me there for some reason. I couldn't care less about all the flavors we could choose from. Just give me a yellow cake with vanilla icing and I'm fine."

"Boy, don't I remember those times. I was just like you. I told my wife to go and take care of everything and I'll just meet her at the altar. And guess what she did?"

"What?"

"She grabbed me by my ear and dragged me to the venue, the floral shop, the tuxedo place, the catering place, and the bakery that made our cake. The only place I didn't go was to the bridal shop when she picked out her gown. And, boy, was I happy."

I chuckled. "You're a funny dude, Tim."

"So, how much has this wedding set you back thus far?"

"Our initial budget was fifty thousand. But by the time this is over, I'm gonna probably fork out one hundred thousand."

"Wow! That's a lot of money. Do you know my wedding only cost us ten thousand?"

"That was what? Over 15 years ago?"

"It was. . . ."

Before Tim could finish his sentence, my cell phone started ringing again. I looked at the caller ID. "This is the call we've been waiting for," I told him, and answered the call.

"Hello," I said.

"The check cleared this morning," Amy started off saying.

"That was quick," I replied with enthusiasm.

"We knew it wasn't gonna take long."

"So, did you withdraw some cash?" I got quick to the point.

"Yes, we did."

"Did you get what we asked you?"

"Yes."

"All right. Sounds good. Could you meet me at the Harris Teeter grocery store in about forty-five minutes?"

"Yes."

"Okay, great. See you then," I said cheerfully, and disconnected the call. "That was Amy. The couple that lives on Lancaster."

"Yeah."

"Their check cleared this morning. We have eight thousand coming our way."

"I thought we agreed to get twenty-five grand on that one."

"We did. Remember, they gave us eight a month after the fire? They are giving us eight more today. And then I'm going to have them give us the last nine next week."

"Oh, okay, I remember now," Tim said.

"Has the old guy from Lake Edward called you back yet?"

"Last time I talked to him, he said that he was still waiting on his check."

"Hasn't it been over four months now?" Tim seemed worried.

"Yeah, and something's telling me that he already got the check and is holding out on us."

"You might wanna give him a call."

"Why don't we just stop by there later tonight?"

"Let's do that," I agreed, and then we dapped each other a handshake and headed into the fire station.

———————

I drove the fire truck to the grocery store, while Tim, my sister, Alayna, our other firefighter, Jesse, and a volunteer named Paul sat in the other sections of the truck. As soon as the truck stopped, everyone climbed out. "Hey, Alayna, you got the grocery list?" I asked her as we all headed across the parking lot.

"Yep, I sure do."

"All right, well, I'm gonna meet y'all inside," I announced as I made a detour in another direction of the parking lot. Tim knew where I was going and gave me a head nod.

I searched the parking lot for Amy's car and finally saw it parked eleven cars away. She and her husband, Mitch, were sitting in the car, waiting for me, as I approached it. I smiled as I walked toward them. And as soon as I got within a few feet of the driver's-side door, I greeted the husband first, because he was the driver.

"How are you doing?" I asked and extended a handshake.

"I'm good, and you?" Mitch replied, and shook my hand.

I leaned over into the driver's-side window and spoke to Amy, who was sitting on the passenger side of the car. "How are you over there?"

She smiled. "I'm great. Beautiful day out."

"I can't agree more."

The husband held a white envelope toward the window and I reached over and grabbed it. "This is the second installment you asked us for. You'll get the other nine next week."

I took the envelope and pushed it down in my front right pocket. "Thank you very much," I said. "Have you guys started the repairs yet?" I asked, making idle conversation. It would've been rude to take the money and just leave.

"We've got a contractor working on it as we speak," Mitch said.

"Did they say how long it's gonna take?" I wondered aloud.

"The back porch will take a week. The back bedroom will take ten days," he answered.

"That's not too bad," I replied.

"I think we could've gotten it done sooner. But Mitch wants to be cheap and this crew doesn't work fast," Amy interjected.

"Hold up, little lady. There is nothing wrong with being cheap," I commented, and laughed.

"I keep telling her, saving a buck here and there will go a long way," Mitch announced.

"I agree with you one hundred percent," I said, and then smiled at them both. I looked down at my watch purposely, so I could give them a reason that I had to run off. "I could do this all day, folks. But I'm gonna have to run in this grocery store and get a few things for the fire station."

"Oh, well, don't let us hold you. Take care of your business and we'll call you next week," Mitch insisted.

"Sounds good. Talk to you folks then," I replied, tapped on the hood of their car, and then walked off.

The moment I entered the grocery store, I searched the aisle for Tim. I finally found him near the deli department. "I got the money."

"Were they acting nervous like they did the first time?"

"No, they were acting pretty calm this time."

"Did you count it?"

"No. I just stuck it in my pocket and came in here."

"Come on, let's go in the men's bathroom and count it," Tim instructed me. "I'll be right back," he told the deli worker, and then walked off. I followed in his footsteps. As soon as we entered the bathroom, I made sure that we were there alone. And when I realized that we were by ourselves, I took the money out of the envelope and began to count. When I got to the end, I noticed that we were short five hundred dollars. This pissed Tim off. "Get on the phone and call their ass now." I could almost see steam coming from his ears as he watched me dial the phone number.

"Hello," I said immediately after Amy answered the phone.

"Yes?"

"You know you guys shorted us five hundred dollars?" I informed her. She fell silent. "Hello," I said once again.

"Yeah, I'm here."

"Did you hear what I said?"

"You said it was short?" she asked.

"Yes, five hundred."

"Hello," I heard her husband's voice say.

"Hey, Mitch, we're short five hundred dollars."

"Are you sure? I counted it myself. I was sure I put eight thousand in the envelope."

"There's only seventy-five hundred in here."

"I'm sorry about that. Can I add it to next week's final payment?"

Livid from his question, I put them on mute and folded my phone into the palm of my hand. "He asked if he could add the other five hundred to the last installment for next week?" I asked Tim.

Tim looked like he wanted to punch the wall. But he remained calm and said okay after waiting about five seconds.

"Yeah, Mitch, next week is fine. But make sure it's ninety-five hundred instead of nine thousand," I told him.

"Will do," he said, and then the phone went dead. I placed the phone back inside my pocket and looked at Tim.

"He's full of shit and he knows it," Tim hissed. He was seething.

"Look, we'll take three thousand seven hundred fifty each. And look at it like this, after next week, we don't have to deal with him anymore."

Tim took his portion of the money and handed me the envelope with the rest. I shoved it down into my pocket and gave him a pat on the back. "It's not the end of the world," I commented, and then exited the bathroom. He followed a couple of seconds later.

Back in the store, I found Alayna with a basket full of groceries and a list of items that she still needed to get. So I helped her. During out trip down the bread aisle, we began to reminisce about our father and his contribution as the city's fire chief before his untimely death. "Pop was the best fire chief this city has ever seen," I started off saying. "Everyone, from the community leaders to the citizens, loved him."

"I know," she said, and smiled proudly.

"Do you know about all the food drives he used to organize?"

"Of course, I do. He had us both there and volunteering."

"What about the toy drives! It was his mission to make sure every child in the city of Virginia Beach have a toy under their Christmas tree."

"Do you remember when he invited those homeless people to our house on Thanksgiving that one time?" Alayna reminded me.

I smiled. "Yeah, I remember that. Mom wasn't too happy about it."

"He's the real reason why I joined the fire department, and for lots of other recruits too," Alayna admitted.

"Absolutely. He was my reason for signing up too. Our dad was a good man."

"Yep. He sure was," Alayna agreed.

"What are you two youngsters talking about?" Tim asked as he approached us.

"My dad," Alayna answered in a boastful way.

"Oh, Chief Riddick. The most respected man in the city of Virginia Beach," Tim acknowledged.

"Yeah, he was your boss too."

"Yes, and sometimes a pain in my ass," Tim commented, and then he chuckled. "He meant well though. He was definitely a good man. And he taught me everything I know."

"He taught us all," I added.

"I wish he was here now," Alayna said aloud.

"If he was, he would be so proud of you," Tim insisted.

"I tell her that all the time," I agreed.

"Got enough food in that grocery cart?" a cop, who came out of nowhere, asked. He was a white cop dressed in uniform. Tim chuckled loudly and started walking toward the cop, and that's when I knew that they knew each other. Alayna and I looked at one another and hunched our shoulders.

"What's going on, buddy? Haven't seen you in ages," Tim told the cop after he embraced him and patted him on his back.

"It's been, what, fifteen years or more?" the cop asked.

"Yep, more like twenty years," Tim corrected him.

"I married my college sweetheart. Relocated to Florida, where she was from, and after thirteen years of that, we grew apart, got a divorce, and I came back here."

"How long have you been back in Virginia?"

"Four years."

After a few words into their conversation, Tim realized that he hadn't introduced Bobby, his cop friend, to Alayna and me, so he turned his attention toward us. He introduced me first and then Alayna. We both smiled, shook his hand, and then they carried on. We excused ourselves to continue shopping, while they continued to catch up.

"Sounds like they've been knowing each other for a long time," Alayna mentioned as we pushed the grocery cart away from them.

"Somehow I'm getting a weird feeling that he didn't just bump into him. It almost feels like he knew we were all standing on that aisle before he walked onto it."

"You think he was watching us?"

"It wouldn't surprise me if he was."

Alayna chuckled. "You're paranoid. Let's go and finish shopping."

Printed in the USA
CPSIA information can be obtained
at www.ICGtesting.com
CBHW010548201023
1423CB00005B/23